Classic
Political
Clangers

Classic
Political
Clangers

David Mortimer

ROBSON BOOKS

First published in the United Kingdom in 2006 by
Robson Books,
151 Freston Road
London
W10 6TH

An imprint of Anova Books Company Ltd

ISBN 1 86105 929 9

A CIP catalogue record for this title is available from the British Library.

Typeset by SX Composing DTP, Rayleigh, Essex
Printed by Creative Print & Design (Wales), Ebbw Vale

www.anovabooks.com

Contents

Classic Political Clangers

Classic Political Clangers

This book is dedicated to every would-be politician who ever stood for office, whether in the local council or at Westminster, and failed to be elected. Congratulations. You spared the rest of us a lot of grief.

There have been many attempts to define politicians, but most agree that an unwavering belief in the brilliance of their own pronouncements comes high on the list of attributes. Despite the usefulness of the internet, the British Newspaper Library remains one of the very best places in which to pin down what they really said while being reminded of the lunacies sometimes perpetrated by their manic alter egos, the gentlemen of the press. Inspiration for the occasional piece has also been found in some books recommended to those who delight in the rich, varied and occasionally crooked characters to be found swimming in the political pond: John Sergeant's *Give me Ten Seconds,* Matthew Parris's *Great Parliamentary Scandals,* and Neil Hamilton's *Great Political Eccentrics.*

Foreword

What is the oldest profession in the world? As a time-honoured question, it ranks alongside the one about the chicken and the egg. How can we be sure that politics outranks prostitution in longevity? If we could keep only one, it's a racing certainty that it wouldn't be politics we would vote for. Nevertheless, we can be grateful to politicians for one thing: they have been dropping clangers with interesting, and sometimes hilarious, regularity since the first scribe laboriously chiselled their doings on a stone tablet. And what, we may well ask ourselves, was that earnest scribe up to? He was establishing the third-oldest profession: that of the spin-doctor. Far from being a new phenomenon, Tony Blair and Alastair Campbell are merely the latest in a very long line of those jostling the prostitutes to claim the imprimatur of antiquity for their endeavours.

'Being a politician is a poor profession, but being a public servant is a noble one,' said Herbert Hoover, president of the United States from 1928 to 1932. Because he was in office when Wall Street crashed in 1929, precipitating the Great Depression, history has remembered Hoover more harshly than he deserves. Apart from being an energetic and outward-looking politician, he was a notable rarity in refusing to take payment or salary for any of the many public offices he held (except one, for which the law required him to be paid, on which occasion he gave the money away). Alas, for every Hoover, there seem – in the public perception, at least – to be a dozen Richard Nixons and Spiro Agnews only too ready to cheat and cozen in order to retain power or to profit from its perks. They in turn command the allegiance of place men whose jobs depend upon their masters' continuation in power, and who are therefore ready to leak any item or turn the truth of any action upside-down in order to persuade the voters that black is white.

Their mistake is consistently to underestimate the perception of those they seek to suborn in this way. 'As ever, the people are ahead of the politicians.' Who said that? Astonishingly, it was a politician, and not any old politician; it was Tony Blair, Britain's beloved leader, who continued, 'We always think as a political class that people, unconcerned with the daily obsession of politics, may not understand it, may not see its subtleties and complexities. But, ultimately, people always see more clearly than us, precisely because they are not daily obsessed with it.' He is right.

Moreover, in its ability to sniff out the false and hypocritical, the electorate has – in Western societies, at least – the ever-eager media to help it do so. The press, radio and television have so thoroughly promoted (and, occasionally, overplayed) their role as watchdogs of the public interest that those who stalk the corridors of power with less than blameless intent are aware that they do so at their peril – or so one would have thought. Yet, despite Tony Blair's dicta, the ability of the average politician to regard himself or herself as superior to other beings, and in possession of wisdom that they neither possess nor comprehend, is so great that hubris or greed seems regularly to dull the antennae with which they ought to apprehend danger. Hence the regular supply of clangers that they let fall.

This little book celebrates some of the incompetent, red-faced or trouserless moments with which politicians of all shades have appalled or delighted observers from mid-Victorian times to the present day. Had it been a book devoted to actors, performers or sportsmen and sportswomen, one might have wished to spare them embarrassment, on the grounds that they were seeking our pleasure and entertainment when the mishap occurred. Can one be so readily forgiving towards politicians? Since I'm confident of the response that most readers would give, I won't even attempt my own.

The Common Man Insists On Dropping His Own Clangers

Henry VIII, Charles I and after, 1509–1850

Errors of political judgement – clangers, if we're to be blunt about it – pass through different ages, as do most things. In the Good Old Days of BMP (Before Modern Politics) only emperors and kings perpetrated them, but, just like Tony Blair, they were never wrong and therefore someone else had to be found to take the blame. This is where the common man came in handy – often with some brevity. It being necessary for kings and emperors to enjoy themselves somehow, usually by fighting battles or spending weeks on end hunting, they tended to employ other people to carry out whatever policy they had concocted in brief moments of respite from sticking boars and slaughtering foot soldiers from armoured horses. When the policy manifestly came unstuck, it was only to be expected that the chap who'd been told to carry it out must have been to blame and he therefore found himself swinging gently in the wind at the end of a rope, or minutely examining the floorboards as he crouched over a chopping block.

England endured a tediously long period of its history – 261 years to be precise – under a procession of Kings unimaginatively called Henry. Of these, number VIII – the one whose size matched the Roman numerals encumbering his name – triumphantly mastered the art of pinning the blame on anyone but himself. Henry had three great ambitions: (i) to be married as often as possible, (ii) to be as rich as possible and (iii) to be head of as many things as possible, and preferably everything. He employed Cardinal Wolsey, who was the son of a butcher and therefore highly expendable if the need arose (as it did), to see to it. Alas, Wolsey failed to persuade the Pope that it was a good idea to let Henry try out a new wife when the king was already married to the sister of the king of Spain, who happened to have entered Rome with an army at that very moment and taken the Pope prisoner. Henry saw at once that it wasn't *his* policy but one that Wolsey must have talked him into when he wasn't listening properly. Rather cleverly, Wolsey managed to die under his own steam before the executioner got hold of him, so in his place Henry installed a chap called Thomas Cromwell, who was younger and fitter and therefore likely to live long enough to be properly executed when the right moment came.

To everyone's surprise, Cromwell turned out to be a very efficient civil servant and for a few years managed things terribly well, making Henry head of the English Church and filling his treasure chest with loot pinched from the monasteries, thus fulfilling ambitions (ii) and (iii) and leaving Henry ample time to sample the pleasures of (i). Divesting himself of his first wife, Henry proceeded rapidly through wives two and three and got ready to welcome number four, as hand-picked by Cromwell, but that was where things came unstuck – or, rather, Cromwell's head did.

In his anxiety to apply the kind of spin that would guarantee the king's satisfaction, Cromwell commissioned a portrait of wife number four that rather over-egged the pudding, or, at any rate, Anne of Cleves' face, which somewhat resembled a pudding. At the very moment when he might have anticipated an index-linked pension and a mention in the Honours List, Cromwell found himself centre stage on Tower Green and face to face – albeit briefly – with the executioner. Today he would probably have been despatched for back-to-back interviews with Jeremy Paxman and John Humphrys, but this is the age of PMP (post-modernist politics) and today's powers-that-be are less merciful than those in Tudor times.

A hundred years or so later, Charles I dropped one of the major clangers in British history and, with it, his head. He convinced himself that God had told him he could do whatever he liked. He explained this patiently and at length to anybody who would listen, which turned out to be fewer people than he'd hoped. Indeed, he spent so much time talking about it, and so little listening to anyone else, that he failed to notice the Common Man not only getting a bit obstreperous but also fairly rich.

Charles needed money, and the wealthy so-and-so's who sat in Parliament wouldn't lend him any, however patiently he explained that it was God's orders that they should cough up. So he decided to take them prisoner until they did – a splendid idea if you can manage it properly but a bit of a clanger if you bungle it, which is what happened. Before you could say 'divine right of kings', armies were tramping all over England, and even over bits of Ireland and Scotland. And, blow me down, the Common Man's side won after extra time – seven years of it, to be precise.

From this point on, it was downhill all the way for the monarchy as far as absolute power was concerned. Soon, ordinary mortals were putting their foot in it with as much zeal as their royal predecessors had ever done. The eighteenth century saw the introduction of a weird creature called a 'prime minister', who presided over strangely named clangers like the War of Jenkins' Ear, the South Sea Bubble (a very British, half-hearted precursor of the Wall Street Crash of 1929 but one that caused the chattering classes of the day much entertainment) and, most famously of all, the loss of the American Colonies. Even today we're still trying to decide whether this last clanger was a Good Thing, a Bad Thing or Just One of Those Things.

By the middle of the nineteenth century, the Reform Bills of 1832 and 1867 had widened the electorate and broadened the base from which members of Parliament could be drawn. With the growth of the railway network, newspapers bearing fact and opinion could be distributed around the country at some speed, and education was on the verge of being expanded to increase the numbers of those who could take an interest in what was going on in London and elsewhere in the world. In short, everything was coming together nicely to guarantee a rapid growth rate for the political clanger.

The Railway King Hits The Buffers

George Hudson's Accounting Practices Are Found To Be Faulty (1849)

'The nineteenth century was a time of many great inventions and thoughts,' wrote a 21st-century lad. Then, after sucking the end of his pencil thoughtfully, he contributed to the anthology of schoolboy howlers by adding, 'The invention of the steamboat caused a network of rivers to spring up. Samuel Morse invented a code of telepathy. Louis Pasteur invented a cure for rabbis. Charles Darwin was a naturalist who wrote *Organ of the Species*. And Karl Marx became one of the Marx brothers.' He might also have added, 'George Hudson invented a way of making money out of railways' – a statement that might have had modern politicians sitting up and taking notice, but for the fact that George Hudson's methods of making money, while perhaps not on a par with those of Robert Maxwell 140 years later, were still distinctly on the naughty side.

We're now so used to the speed at which technology advances, spewing forth gadgets and inventions on an almost daily basis, that it's difficult to appreciate the near-hysteria occasioned by the invention and development of steam-powered railways in the second quarter of the nineteenth century. For people accustomed to being conveyed slowly on horseback or in horse-drawn carriages, the idea of being able to go from A to B at the heady speed of 30 miles an hour was dizzying, if not downright dangerous.

'Railway mania' this new craze was christened, and George Hudson, MP for Sunderland, not to mention lord mayor of York and deputy lieutenant for Durham, was its arch-priest. Starting out as a draper, in 1828 Hudson inherited £30,000, some of which he invested in one of the earliest 'iron railroads', the North Midland. It was the success of this speculation that sent him bowling merrily down the tracks.

Hudson's boom years were 1846–9, when he seemed to have interests in every other railway company – so much so, indeed, that by the time of his collapse he controlled lines stretching from Berwick-on-Tweed on the Scottish border to Bristol in the west country. Almost one-third of the entire British rail network, then consisting of about 5000 miles, was in Hudson's grasping fingers. But, even taking into account the money to be made from charging goods and passengers for quick passage around the country, how was he financing it all? In real terms, the building and running of railways was little cheaper then than now. No problem as far as Hudson was concerned – keep money on the move.

By now known as the 'Railway King', he became chairman of the York Union Bank, through which he borrowed heavily in the City, using the capital to pay dividends to his shareholders. In one case (that of his Eastern Counties company) he paid dividends in this way of more than £320,000 – over £20 million by present-day standards – in one four-year period.

For many years, Hudson made life simple for himself by failing to notice that he had no proper written accounts, let alone audited ones. Enquiries as to when the magic figures might be seen generally met with a bluff and reassuring comment along the lines of 'Don't thi worry, sir. They're all in me head', and as long as he gave the appearance of being a financial wizard, people were willing to go along with this. Inevitably, there were many panting to climb aboard this express train to wealth and although you might clutch your brow in disbelief, the politicians of the day were no exception. No fewer than 155 MPs awoke each morning to ruminate contentedly over their eggs and toast that they were directors of this or that railway company. It helped, of course, that the Railway King had shelled out £9,000 (well over half a million smackers today) to keep his fellow MPs compliant.

Things began to unravel at the start of 1849, and once the process had started, the end came quickly. What finished Hudson was his inability or unwillingness to build a direct east-coast route to London from the Northeast. While his passengers were being taken on a zig-zag journey from Newcastle via, say, Derby and Birmingham, his competitors were busy working out what a straight line was and laying down tracks forthwith. Hudson's belated attempt to follow suit came too late. Awkward questions began to be asked and two of his own companies set up independent committees to investigate what was going on. Too much for comfort, it transpired.

It was the bribery of MPs, however, that really raised hackles in Westminster. Then, as now, a fellow could be a swindler and a bounder and have a chance of escaping censure within the august walls of the Commons provided his behaviour there was impeccable. Terminological inexactitudes uttered before one's fellow members, however, or payments that fell out of back pockets in the debating chamber itself were another matter, and Hudson was called upon to explain himself. He couldn't and his empire collapsed before his disbelieving gaze.

Despite his financial ruination, Hudson fought to remain an MP and, strangely, succeeded in hanging on in the Commons for another ten years before losing his seat. While understanding only too well that his status afforded him protection from the law, he nevertheless took care always to remove himself to France when parliament wasn't sitting, and when the voters eventually threw him out he retired there, permanently and penniless.

The Tailor Who Hadn't Learned To Sew

Andrew Johnson Gives A Masterclass In How Not To Run The USA (1865–9)

They were an erratic lot, the first few presidents of the United States. They began well, with aristocrats like Thomas Jefferson and John Quincy Adams running the show with high-minded ideals and administrative skill, but when the Common Man got in on the act he began to prove himself a bit too common, or else regrettably lacking in stamina to see the job through.

The ninth president was William Henry Harrison, known to all and sundry from his army days as 'Old Tippecanoe'. On hanging up his sword, he tried his hand at being a diplomat, but his outspoken military approach quickly got him into trouble. (He once told Simon Bolivar he was a fool – not the best way to win friends for your country). Instead, he decided to be a politician, eventually – and rather to his surprise – making it to the presidency. So excited was he by this upturn in his fortunes that he promptly expired in April 1841, exactly one month after taking office. His record brevity in the office stands to this day.

The twelfth president, Zachary Taylor, or 'Old Rough and Ready', nevertheless made a valiant bid to claim Harrison's record. After dinner on Independence Day, 4 July 1850, precisely sixteen months after taking office, he rose from the table clutching his stomach, declined dramatically upon the carpet and died five days later. Ever since Americans have nurtured a fascination for conspiracy theories, and in next to no time the whisper went around that Old Rough and Ready had been poisoned. Not until his body was exhumed and examined in 1991 could the rumour be laid finally to rest, when it was established that he had died of cholera.

But this is by the by. Who knows? Old Tippecanoe and Old Rough and Ready might have gone on to become memorable presidents. When, in April 1865, at the close of the Civil War, the assassin's bullet felled Abraham Lincoln, one of America's greatest incumbents of that office, it catapulted into the presidency the just-appointed vice-president, Andrew Johnson, in many people's opinion the worst president the USA has ever endured and one who came within a whisker of impeachment. The sole reason Lincoln had chosen him as a running mate was because he was a southerner, the only one from the secessionist states willing and available to serve the administration in Washington during the Civil War. Lincoln believed Johnson would be valuable in helping to heal the nation and bring the South back into the fold once the hostilities were over. The first and last tailor America has ever selected as president, Johnson managed to fashion a Union suit whose trousers repeatedly fell down.

He got off to an unpromising start with his vice-presidential inauguration speech the month before Lincoln's demise, when he fortified himself rather too well with spirits and produced an oration incomprehensible to many and too long for everybody. A week or two later, he suddenly found himself president and in possession of wartime emergency powers – including sole command of the army – that meant he could effectively rule single-handed until the legislature was recalled in December 1865, eight months ahead. Faced with the most daunting task, and the greatest opportunity, that any president before or since has ever had, he metaphorically sprang into the saddle and made for the horizon at full gallop before Congress could reconvene and rob him of his glory.

Unfortunately for his chances of being acclaimed a hero when Congress finally reclaimed its rightful place in the scheme of things, Johnson overlooked one or two crucial points. First, he was a southerner, and the soon-to-be-returned legislators were northerners, the people who had won the long and bloody war. Secondly, one of the great issues over which so much blood had been spilled was the eradication of slavery in the southern states and the emancipation of the slaves. Thirdly, the northern armies had not been called the Unionists for nothing; they had, above all else, fought for the union of all states.

It was not, therefore, the most considered thing in the world to rush through, off his own bat, the right of the southern states to draft their own constitutions, elect their own officers and decide for themselves how (which, in reality, meant whether or not) to abolish slavery.

Needless to say, the southern states thought Christmas had come early and promptly complied with the bits of the new laws that they liked but conspicuously failed to do anything constructive about abolishing slavery. Their elected representatives duly arrived, bright-eyed and bushy-tailed, in Washington for the first sitting of the restored Congress, probably thinking how reassuring it was to have a man of good sense in the White House after that single-minded bigot Lincoln. But now that it was back in business, Congress had ideas that were very different from Johnson's and refused to allow the southern representatives a seat in the house. In 1866, it passed new laws to protect the ex-slaves in the South, and in 1867 it set aside the state governments there, sending in the army to supervise matters until such time as equal political and civil rights had been established.

At every turn, Johnson tried to hamper or overturn their efforts, especially in the matter of controlling the army, of which he remained nominal commander-in-chief. Indeed, he used his veto so many times that it became almost too hot to handle, and Congress eventually voted to veto the president's veto.

The final crunch came in February 1868, when Johnson sacked the Secretary for War in seeming violation of the law, whereupon the House of Representatives impeached the president and he was tried by the Senate. Not for the last time in America, it was a profitable period for the lawyers and, thanks to the ability of his legal team to obfuscate the issues, Johnson scraped out of his pickle by just one vote. He remained in office for the remainder of his term, but he had learned a painful lesson and stayed tactfully quiet.

Queen Victoria Finds Herself Faintly Amused

The Fall Of Sir Charles Dilke (1886)

In the 1980s, certain politicians were said to be fond of advocating a return to Victorian standards. If so, they clearly hadn't done their homework very well and obviously failed to understand that human nature remains pretty much the same throughout all eras. We get away with whatever we can, hoping to avoid exposure, and the Victorians were very little different from ourselves. The paradox of the Dilke affair of 1885–6 was that its protagonist was almost certainly entirely innocent of the scandal that ruined his political career.

Sir Charles Dilke was a rising star of British politics in the 1880s, and by 1883 he was president of the Local Government Board in Prime Minister William Gladstone's Liberal administration. Dilke was widely seen as a PM-in-waiting, should the Grand Old Man ever see fit to retire, but the collapse of any such hope can be dated with precision to 19 July 1885, when he was confronted by allegations that he had been misbehaving on a grand scale. Twenty-two-year-old Mrs Virginia Crawford accused him of having affairs not only with her but also with her mother, with his friend Mrs Christina Rogerson and with a girl called Sarah who was one of his maids. Nor did matters stop there; for good measure, Mrs Crawford alleged that he had frequently coerced her into a bed built for three accompanied by a waitress called Fanny Stock, where he had proceeded to teach them 'every French vice'. Not a bad track record for a prominent and radical Liberal to boast – assuming, of course, that there was any truth whatsoever in the allegations.

At this stage of his life Dilke, while admittedly a bit of a ladies' man, was not married, and there was one name on the list to which he could, and did, own up: Mrs Smith, the mother of his accuser. But, according to the ethics of the day, it was acceptable for a man in his position to have such an affair, provided one remained discreet about it. For the Victorians, it was divorce, or being associated with divorce, that was unforgivable.

Dilke recognised immediately not only that the list of his supposed amours was too long for Victorian sensibilities to stomach but that it was probably designed to create a smokescreen under which Mrs Crawford could hide from her husband the affair that she was really conducting with a man named Captain Forster. Mr Crawford, considerably older than his wife, had hired detectives to follow her and establish the identity of the lover he was certain she had, and her list of accusations against Dilke might have been launched out of her fear that her husband was getting too near the truth. What Dilke could not be sure of was whether the plot was politically contrived by those anxious to see this radical republican knocked out of contention for high office after the forthcoming election. Queen Victoria was notorious for her refusal to be amused, but the sight of a republican being hounded from office may have caused a faint smile to cross her face in private.

Whatever the motivational permutations, Mr Crawford sought a divorce from his wife, citing her confession as proof of her infidelity. Dilke attended the divorce hearing, held in February 1886, as a possible witness, but was not called. Despite the lack of any evidence, the divorce was granted, a decision that automatically implied that Dilke had to be guilty, as stated by Mrs Crawford. The press had a field day, led by the *Pall Mall Gazette* under the editorship of WT Stead, self-appointed guardian of the nation's morals and a figure who was not widely mourned when he went down with the *Titanic* 26 years later. While Stead occasionally picked good causes to fight for, he was as capable of the scurrilous as any modern muck-raking tabloid editor, and he launched a campaign calling for Dilke to clear his name. The MP responded by applying successfully for a second hearing of the divorce application before it became absolute. In the meantime, he and his lawyer had unearthed proof of Virginia Crawford's adultery with Captain Forster and had also located Fanny Stock, who flatly denied the three-in-a-bed stories.

The second hearing took place in July 1886, in a courtroom packed with public and journalists. Once again, Dilke was there only as a witness, which meant that his lawyer wouldn't be allowed to cross-examine Mrs Crawford. The fact that any hope of clearing his name rested on being able to prove that he had never slept with an individual whom he could not call as a witness was bad enough, but worse, he was the first to be called into the witness box, allowing Mrs Crawford and her lawyers to hear what he had to say. This meant that, when she was called, she could deny whatever he said without being required to undergo cross-examination, although her adultery with Captain Forster was at last admitted.

It took the jury precisely fifteen minutes to reach a verdict: the divorce stood. This left Dilke's position as unclear as it had been before the trial. He was neither palpably guilty, yet he was not cleared either, and in a society of rumour and innuendo it was the final blow to his political career. He resigned as the MP for Chelsea.

Five years later, Dilke's friends and supporters uncovered evidence that Virginia Crawford's affair with Captain Forster had been far more intense than had ever been admitted, and that she had had other lovers, including (in company with her sister) medical students from the nearby teaching hospital. Historians have subsequently concluded that Dilke was almost certainly framed and, although he did return to the Commons as MP for the Forest of Dean, he never again held office.

Careless Mistake Or Ruthless Decision?

De Valera Sends Michael Collins To Negotiate With Lloyd George (1921)

Ask any Irishman to name the leading figures in Eire's struggle for independence from the British in the period between 1916 and 1921 and the chances are that Eamon de Valera and Michael Collins will top the list. Both men were active in the 1916 Easter Rising, but thereafter de Valera followed a more political path while Collins, although a member of Sinn Fein's executive committee, continued to regard himself primarily as a soldier. The charismatic 'Big Fellow', as Collins was known, led his Irish Volunteers in a campaign of violence against anything representing British authority in Ireland, including the police and the army.

The response of the British was to send in the notorious Black and Tans, an army unit primed to spread terror throughout southern Ireland, and the British generals gave their prime minister, David Lloyd George, some blunt advice on the Irish position: 'Go all out or get out.' They understood very well that the situation was so extreme that it could be contained, if at all, only by all-out repression. In such circumstances, Lloyd George knew that some form of negotiated settlement had to be reached.

In July 1921, therefore, a truce was signed. De Valera had been president of Sinn Fein since October 1917 and, from 1919, also president of the Dail, the self-proclaimed government of the Irish Republic. Naturally enough, therefore, it was he who led the Irish delegation to

14

London for exploratory talks that broke down almost before they had begun. Lloyd George was prepared to recognise a self-governing Eire, but only within the framework of the British Empire, whereas de Valera would accept nothing less than complete independence. Moreover, then as now, the issue of the six counties of Ulster hung over everything. De Valera insisted on the independence of the whole of Ireland, and this – as modern history has shown us all too clearly – could be achieved only within a very long timescale, if at all.

By September 1921, de Valera had been elected president of the Irish Republic, a position and government unrecognised by Britain, of course, but one that gave him sovereign status in the eyes of his own people. Lloyd George refused to negotiate on such a basis, but offered to resume talks on how Ireland might fulfil its self-governing aspirations.

De Valera, the one Irish political negotiator of some experience, could see that neither a fully-fledged republic nor a united Ireland could be wrung from the British and refused to go to London. But to decline any further discussions would be to leave himself open to attack from the many people who believed that any political progress in the short term could be only to Ireland's benefit and would inevitably lead to further concessions later on. He therefore nominated Michael Collins and Arthur Griffith to confront Lloyd George, the wiliest politician of his generation. Neither Griffith nor Collins wanted to go, the latter very reasonably protesting that he was a soldier, not a politician. The issue was put before the Cabinet and the vote was tied, leaving the casting vote to de Valera, who decreed that they had to go. One historian has since called this 'the worst single decision of de Valera's life', but one is entitled to ask if it was an error honestly made or a deliberate ploy to weaken, if not remove, the influence of the popular Collins.

Reluctantly, Collins and Griffith set off with the rest of their delegation to London, where they spent three difficult and trying months trying to withstand the arguments of their experienced British counterparts and settle differences of opinion within their own party. Collins recognised the reality that de Valera could not or would not acknowledge – that a united Ireland, including Ulster, was not an achievable outcome in the shorter term – but he also recognised another reality: that to refuse any settlement would lead inevitably to all-out war in which many Irish lives would be lost. Reluctantly, he concluded that a step towards independence was the lesser of two evils. As he signed the Anglo-Irish Treaty, he said, with grim understanding, 'I tell you, I have signed my own death warrant.' He was right.

The treaty was accepted in the Dail by 64 votes to 57. (It goes almost without saying that de Valera's was one of the votes against ratification.) Ireland and its freedom fighters split in comparable proportions, between those who saw the treaty as 'the freedom to win freedom' and the diehards who wanted everything at once or not at all.

Collins tried desperately to avoid the tragedy of civil war, but to no avail. On 12 August 1922, Arthur Griffith, his co-negotiator of the Treaty, died of a massive heart attack brought on by the strain of it all. Ten days later, Michael Collins himself met the end he had prophesied, gunned down at Beal na mBlath ('the Mouth of Flowers') in County Cork. He was 32 years old. For three days his body lay in state in Dublin and many thousands filed past his coffin to pay him a tearful farewell.

De Valera was prime minister of the Irish republic four times between 1937 and 1957 and president of the republic from 1959–73. He died at the age of 92 in 1975. Did he ever regret his decision to send Griffith and Collins to London in 1921? Probably not.

Who Will Buy My Beautiful Dukedoms?

Lloyd George And The Honours Scandal (1921–2)

'Five hundred men chosen at random from the ranks of the unemployed,' as Lloyd George thundered so memorably from the safety of the Commons. On this occasion, he was pouring his scorn on the denizens of the House of Lords – unelected peers – as they tried to block his reforming budget of 1909, and one could reasonably deduce from his remarks that he did not place great value either on their lordships' judgements or their persons – not, that is, until, in the wake of the financial drain of World War I, he found himself in need of ready cash.

In 1922, a general election loomed on the horizon. At that time, David Lloyd George was the incumbent prime minister of a coalition government of Liberals and Conservatives, but he was not the leader of his own Liberal Party. That post was still held by Herbert Asquith, ousted as PM by Lloyd George in 1916 at one of the lowest points of the war. There was no love lost between the Asquith camp and that of LG; indeed the Liberals were well and truly split, with many party members who would rather see a Tory government than one led by their arch-enemy, and it was this camp, led by Asquith, that held the party's purse strings.

Lloyd George put on his thinking cap and came up with a scheme that was not new but had never before been implemented in the brazen manner he was about to inaugurate. In the past, a willing government had occasionally accepted an inducement here and there to slip a coronet and an ermine cape in the direction of someone who fancied them, but hitherto it had done so only if the recipient had made public benefactions sufficiently honourable to provide a respectable cover story.

Lloyd George had neither the time nor the inclination to bother with such niceties. Possessed of the cunning an aged fox might have envied, his view of human morality was a low one. As Margot Asquith said of him, 'He could not see a belt without hitting below it.' His opinion of those who held peerages was no exception, and given his scant regard for those in the upper chamber – whose power of veto he had helped curtail in 1911 – why not make as much money as possible from trading on other people's sense of self-importance?

A broker was appointed to hawk around titles. This was a man called Maundy Gregory, who had hitherto failed at whatever he had attempted – teaching, acting, playwrighting – but was now to shine in the role for which nature had evidently designed him.

A price list was drawn up. Mere knighthoods were handed out for £10,000 a handle, but baronetcies were hereditary and therefore more expensive. 'I think I might persuade the PM to set you up with one of those, sir, if you could see your way to slipping £30,000 across the desk,' Maundy might well have said, after which he would approach the higher reaches of title-mongering. You want to be a viscount? Possible, but costly, as I'm sure you were expecting, my dear fellow. Shall we say £50,000? Or would you prefer an earldom? It is, after all, somewhat more dignified. Let us enjoy a glass of claret while we think about it. Those with vaulting ambition and really deep pockets could clear their throats and enquire about the prospects of becoming a marquis or, best (and most expensive) of all, a real, live duke.

Not surprisingly, given human greed and self-regard, by the middle of 1922 Lloyd George found his coffers swelled by £2 million, a fair sum even by today's standards but worth very much more then.

Such shameless doings could hardly remain covert, however, and it wasn't long before music halls began to echo with jokes directed at the newly ennobled and London was rechristened 'City of the Dreadful Knights'. From this period dates the catchy line 'Lloyd George knew my father; father knew Lloyd George,' which some recipients of these doubtful honours heard being hummed softly to the tune of 'Onward Christian Soldiers' as they entered a room.

Then, in July 1922, public derision turned to fury when the Honours List was published containing baronetcies for John Drughorn, a shipowner convicted in the middle of the Great War for trading with the enemy; William Vestey, a known tax dodger; and Joseph Robinson, who had just been convicted of defrauding his own sharcholders. Lloyd George was openly derided in a Commons debate and the establishment of a Select Committee was demanded. The prime minister twisted and turned, and it even began to look as if he might survive the onslaught; after all, there were by now rather a lot of recipients of his patronage who would rather the full story did not come out.

Lloyd George's administration was now thoroughly discredited, both in the country and among the Tory coalition partners, and when the Chanak crisis – in which Lloyd George appeared to be inciting war with Turkey – blew up, the Conservatives decided that enough was enough. They were already furious that he had reached a settlement giving home rule to the southern Irish, and now they deserted the coalition. A disillusioned public hounded the Liberals out of office, and in the 80-plus years since they have never again come close to government.

Scraping The Bottom

Horatio Bottomley Tries One Fraud Too Many (1922)

To say that Horatio Bottomley was a nasty piece of work would be to malign other nasty pieces of work. His dominant qualities were a quick wit, a loud voice and an ability to talk anyone else into submission. Applied in the right directions, they might have been valuable, but in the furtherance of Bottomley's self-importance and personal wealth, they were a menace and, to countless small investors, catastrophic.

Bottomley was a self-made man, in every sense of the term. An orphan by the age of nine, he was on the streets by the time he was fourteen, whereupon he found a job as an office boy in a firm of solicitors. Being a quick learner, he was soon taking shorthand notes in the courts, where he picked up an invaluable knowledge of legal jargon that would stand him in good stead when defending himself against the 67 charges of bankruptcy and fraud of which he was to be accused between 1901 and 1905.

In 1885, at the age of 25, Bottomley set up his first company (with shades of Robert Maxwell two generations later, it was a printing and publishing company), which turned out to be a blueprint for most of his subsequent ventures – i.e., a scandal of ripping off other people and allowing the finances to become such a mess that no one could pin the responsibility with any certainty on him. Investors were talked into sinking £250,000 into the company and £85,000 of it simply vanished. Where it had gone, nobody could say for certain, and in court Bottomley – conducting his own defence, as he would always do – managed to persuade the court that it was impossible to lay the blame on him.

Thus encouraged, the bold Horatio turned his attention to gold mines in the far-flung outposts of Australia and South Africa that few, if any, were ever likely to visit. In the course of ten years, he launched around 50 finance and mining companies, accumulating a personal fortune of around £3 million – a vast sum a century ago – on the back of other people's greed and naïvety. As fast as writs were issued against him, he talked his way out of them before the judge and could never be pinned down.

By 1906, Bottomley was ready to take the next step and got himself elected Liberal MP for the London constituency of South Hackney. It didn't stop the writs landing on his doorstep, but he remained unabashed and unconvicted.

The years of World War I saw Bottomley at his inglorious worst. True, he was no longer an MP but he remained, as he was once called, 'a silver-tongued charmer', and was called on to lend his oratorical skills to recruitment drives. He was also paid the princely sum of almost £8,000 a year to write a column about the war effort for the *Sunday Pictorial*, consequently earning the undying contempt of the poor bloody infantry in their shell holes and flooded trenches at the front as he ranted on about the offensive spirit from the comfort of his well-appointed London address.

In 1918, Bottomley re-entered parliament as an independent MP and, still trading on the war, launched the scheme that was, at last, to undo him. Seeing around him the relief and happiness engendered by the end of the 'war to end wars', he sought to capitalise on the mood by devising the Victory Bond Club, whose message seemed to be, 'Invest in trustworthy Horatio's bonds and help to rebuild Britain while earning yourself a bob or two.' Astonishingly, given his career of court appearances in the pre-war years, the gullible masses still believed he'd get it right in the end. At the height of the scheme, £100,000 a day poured in and the queues to invest were so great that the police had to be called in to impose some sort of order.

Naturally enough, given his record, Bottomley promptly pocketed most of the cash, investing some of it in a couple of newspapers and a great deal of the rest in his mistresses and his racehorses. Thousands of small investors, as well as a few larger ones, lost their shirts and, once more, Horatio trod the familiar path to the court in Bow Street. By 1922, however, the mood was more cynical, and this time the Bottomley magic failed to exert its hypnotism. In summing up his own defence, he pointed an outstretched arm to the figure of justice above the court and, with a poetic licence that ignored the fact that the weapon in question was drawn, thundered, 'That sword would drop from its scabbard if you gave a verdict of guilty against me.' The jury scurried out. Risking the Damocletian wrath called down upon their heads they were back in a record-breaking 25 minutes. Bottomley was found guilty – at last – and sent down for seven years.

On his release in 1927, he faced contempt and humiliation. One of his earlier girlfriends got him an appearance at the Windmill Theatre, but he was booed off the stage. By the time of his death in 1933, he was dependent on the charity of the few friends who were prepared to stand by him.

Between A Rock And A Barbarous Relic

Churchill Returns Britain To The Gold Standard (1925)

To any economists reading this book, I apologise for the crude and truncated nature of the following account, but the tedious-sounding problem of the gold standard was crucial to the lives of all our grandparents, even though no more than a handful may ever have known what the wretched thing was.

At the root of the problem was the world's need for a monetary system with a standard economic unit so that trade could proceed without wildly fluctuating rates of exchange between currencies. For centuries, gold had been just the job for this, and as the Industrial Revolution caused the world's trade to expand rapidly in the nineteenth century, it seemed to a number of countries that whoever could sit on the biggest gold reserve was well on the way to becoming Top Nation. Who needed to sail around the world grabbing colonies if you had the loot necessary to control everyone else's business locked up in your own cellar?

Until the Franco-Prussian war of 1870–1, France was doing very well at this game and Paris was the world's major centre of finance and banking. Then it made the big mistake of letting Prussia lay siege to it, at which point, not surprisingly, everyone wanted to get their own gold out of the city and stash it elsewhere. 'Where better than London?' said the British to themselves, thus heralding the era of London as the centre of world power, a state of affairs that they found very comfortable at the time. Then, in 1886, oodles of gold were found lying about in South Africa. As the years passed, careful discussions over a lunch here and a night at the opera there persuaded those who mattered that letting London look after all this South African gold was in everyone's best interests, but then three rather unfortunate things happened, in the following order. First of all was the outbreak of World War I, which got all the major participants heavily in debt and caused a suspension of the gold standard. Secondly, America began to grow rather big and strong and started wondering to itself why a country like Britain, that didn't play baseball, should be running everything. Thirdly, in 1924 South Africa saw the election of a nationalist government under a Boer leader who positively disliked Britain. After some secret prodding by the Americans, he threatened to unhitch the South African currency, the rand, from sterling and send all South African gold to Washington in future, simply because the US of A was back on the gold standard and Britain was not. There was much indignant spluttering in the corridors of power. Did you ever hear of such a thoroughly devious and un-British way of doing things – one, moreover, that would have the unspeakable effect of making America Top Nation! Clearly such an occurrence could not be allowed.

There was an obvious solution, of course: put Britain back on the gold standard. That removed the argument that the South African rand would be better off tied to the dollar instead of sterling. For the rest, through its control over merchant shipping, Britain could ensure that the rates for shipping gold to London were so much lower than those for shipping it to America – well, dash it all, it *is* further, old boy – that it would be positively damaging to send it anywhere else. Simple. Problem solved.

Except for one thing: America had gone back on the gold standard at the pre-war rate. If Britain was to do the same, the pound would be valued at $4.86, a ludicrous level given the decline in British industrial output thanks to the war. Exports would immediately be badly overpriced, trade would be lost, both the public debt and inflation would rise, industry would shrink and jobs would be lost in their many thousands.

The British government, whose chancellor of the exchequer was one

Winston S Churchill, was caught between a rock and a hard place – or 'a barbarous relic', as Maynard Keynes, the gold standard's most implacable enemy, put it. What to do? Either way pointed if not to catastrophe then to something only a little less bad.

Actually, it wasn't the South African threat alone that was nagging at Churchill, who saw well enough the domestic problems that a return to the gold standard would cause. At that time, the German mark – currency of Britain's chief European industrial rival – was in free fall under the Weimar republic, and it was those damnable Americans again – Britain's leading global rivals – who were hatching a plan to rescue the German economy by returning it to a US-led gold standard. Who could tell what evils would befall Britain's financial hegemony and world leadership if those two got together? Churchill must have chewed the ends off a great many cigars as he and the government envisaged the damage a flight of gold from London would do.

Finally, on 28 April 1925, Churchill bit the bullet and announced Britain's return to the gold standard at the pre-war rate of $4.86. To back him up, the Bank of England kept interest rates abnormally high in order to retain London's attractiveness as the place to stash gold, while the British public, its industry and its workforce paid the price. What the cost of the opposite course of action would have been we shall never know and can barely guess. Either way, succeeding generations would probably have labelled it a clanger.

'Go Home And Get A Nice Quiet Sleep'

Neville Chamberlain Declares 'Peace In Our Time' (September 1938)

As ringing clangers go, Neville Chamberlain's belief that he had persuaded Adolf Hitler to shed the hide of a rampaging bull and cloak himself as a lamb echoes down our history like a peal of cathedral bells. Chamberlain belonged to a generation appalled by the muddy slaughter in the trenches of what its members called 'the Great War' and 'the war to end all wars'. To them, almost any price was worth paying to avoid a repetition of such barbarism. On the face of it, the coming generation appeared to accept their beliefs, most famously in the much-publicised Oxford Union debate of 1933 in which the motion that one should be prepared to fight for one's king and country was decisively rejected.

It was evident that the attitude of the British political class was supine. It seemed wholly unwilling to believe that Hitler could have any evil intent, let alone an aspiration to world domination, and never began to understand that a young nation like Germany felt a deep national humiliation about the severity with which it had been treated at the end of the First World War. Germany's leaders believed that they had done no more than agree a truce, rather as though the war had been a high-scoring draw with extra time yet to be played. Only a handful of far-sighted people foresaw that German resentment created the conditions for extremists to whip up nationalistic fervour and precipitate that extra time as surely as day follows night. The economic stagnation with which much of the Western world was afflicted in the 1920s and 1930s provided fertile soil for such extremism.

Meanwhile, the British politicians of the 1930s, with limited resources at their disposal, sought to advance social reform at the expense of rearmament and, with the wholehearted connivance of much of the press, derided as fringe warmongers those who, like Winston Churchill, Anthony Eden, Duff Cooper and Bob Boothby, consistently warned of the dangers that lay ahead. 'The Conservative Party was rotten at the core,' wrote Boothby. 'The Labour and Liberal parties were no better. They made violent pacifist speeches and voted steadily against the miserable Defence Estimates of 1935, 1936, 1937 and 1938.' Across the channel, Adolf Hitler and the Nazis took note of this British refusal to prepare any military opposition to whatever they might choose to do.

Neville Chamberlain was a politician who had enjoyed a meteoric rise through the ranks, having achieved the position of postmaster general within four years of entering the House as an MP in 1918 and chancellor of the exchequer within five, reaching the pinnacle in 1937, when he succeeded Stanley Baldwin as premier and leader of the Conservative Party. By then, even Baldwin – a man who, in Winston Churchill's words, 'occasionally stumbled over the truth, but hastily picked himself up, and hurried on as if nothing had happened' – might have acknowledged in an unguarded moment that what Hitler and the Nazis were up to was threatening, and it was on Baldwin that posterity heaped the greatest blame for his refusal to arrest Britain's military stagnation. It was Chamberlain, though, who reaped the political whirlwind.

By 1937, the Spanish Civil War was in full and brutal flow and Nazi Germany was testing its weaponry in support of Franco's fellow fascists. The following year, Hitler marched into Austria and then provoked a further crisis by announcing to a puzzled and alarmed world that part of Czechoslovakia really belonged to Germany and that the Sudetenland – largely peopled by those who had originally come from Germany, even though they might not realise it – should be 'returned'. If not, he vowed, it would be necessary to go and get it.

27

As the Nazis ratcheted up their demands, Chamberlain travelled to Germany three times in a single month, September 1938, to meet 'Herr Hitler', as he persisted in calling him. 'A way out will now be found,' 'Chips' Channon confided joyfully to his diary when the first such visit was announced. 'Neville, by his imagination and practical good sense, has saved the world.' Yet internal Foreign Office reports of the first two meetings reveal that Hitler had conceded not an inch.

The third meeting, in Munich on 29th of the month, was a four-sided one, with Daladier of France and Mussolini of Italy also present. On the eve of his departure from London, Chamberlain broadcast to the nation and delivered the infamous line, 'How horrible, fantastic, incredible it is that we should be digging trenches and trying on gas-masks here because of a quarrel in a far-away country between people of whom we know nothing!' The unpalatable truth was that Chamberlain's main concern was to prevent war between Britain and Germany, no matter that this left others to the mercy of the Nazis. His statement could hardly have given Hitler a clearer message that the Führer had only to promise non-aggression towards Britain in order to secure compliance.

Modern apologists have suggested that Chamberlain understood the situation only too well but knew that he had to buy time for Britain's military resources to be replenished after the years of neglect in the preceding decade. It is true that, in the same eve-of-visit broadcast, he said, 'If I were convinced that any nation had made up its mind to dominate the world by fear of its force, I should feel that it must be resisted . . . but war is a fearful thing, and we must be very clear before we embark on it that it is really the great issues that are at stake.'

Whatever Chamberlain's motives in Munich, the great majority of the British people were desperate for peace and reassurance. Crowds flocked to meet his plane on his return to London, and were rewarded with the sight of their prime minister waving a piece of paper in the air. 'We regard the agreement signed last night . . . as symbolic of the desire of our two peoples never to go to war with one another again' he told the cheering throng. 'A British Prime Minister has returned from Germany bringing peace with honour. I believe it is peace for our time . . . Go home and get a nice quiet sleep.'

Perhaps a 'nice quiet sleep' was necessary preparation for the efforts that the future would soon demand. Within six months, Germany had occupied Czechoslovakia and Albania and turned its attentions to Poland. Even Chamberlain now saw that, as the Foreign Office had consistently warned following its diplomats' conversations with senior Nazis, 'domination of the world by fear of its force' was precisely what Hitler intended. Eleven months after the prime minister had promised peace in our time, Britain was at war with Germany and aggressive fascism, while Chamberlain's attempts to placate Hitler were labelled 'appeasement'. As Churchill said, 'An appeaser is one who feeds a crocodile hoping it will eat him last,' and to this day the sense of betrayal felt by the British as a result of Chamberlain's failure runs so deep that 'appeasement' remains a term of abuse.

Dame Irene Demands The Raising Of The Hemline

Irene Ward Entertains The Commons (1941)

By sheer weight of numbers, there have been more male than female 'characters' in British parliamentary life, but pound for pound, as it were, the number of women MPs who have left a heavy dent in the chamber's life is every bit as great. For example, one has to think only of the angular Edith Summerskill or the outsized Bessie Braddock – or, of course, Irene Ward, or Dame Irene as she became in 1974.

You might think that it was Mrs Thatcher who introduced the life-sapping handbag to UK political life. Not a bit of it; that honour surely goes to the formidable Dame Irene, who spent at least part of five decades in the Commons before giving the Lords the benefit of her direction for a further six years. Sitting in the chamber, 'she gave the impression of a First World War dreadnought riding at anchor in Scapa Flow,' as Neil Hamilton has memorably described her. She was large, forthright and indomitable, and her handbag could stun a minister as surely as Mrs T's ever did. During a reception held as part of a parliamentary delegation to Nazi Germany in 1936, her voice was heard rising above the momentarily-hushed throng as she addressed Adolf Hitler: 'What absolute bosh you are talking,' she informed the man who intended to rule the world.

Among Dame Irene's more memorable moments was one that turned out to be not quite as effective as she'd intended but brought much delight to its almost entirely male audience. In the early part of World War II,

Britain was desperately short of nearly everything, including the blue serge required for naval uniforms. With the limited supplies available, the question was, which came first – the clothing of the male Royal Navy ratings aboard ship or that of the female Women's Royal Naval Service – the Wrens – supporting them on land? It hardly needs to be said which way Dame Irene was inclined.

The First Lord of the Admiralty pondered the matter and, on being called by her to give his decision, rose and stated that, after much thought, etc., etc., he had decided that the men took priority. His reasons for this decision did not, to Dame Irene, contain the clear and unanswerable logic that could deflect her from her own opinion. She rose to the full height of her ample six-foot figure, closely resembling Collingwood's *Royal Sovereign* breaking the line under full sail at Trafalgar, and boomed, 'Is the minister seriously telling me that the skirts of the Wrens must be held up until the needs of the men have been satisfied?'

'Yes, We Have No Bananas; We Have No Bananas Today'

The Post-War Government Shows How Not To Manage A Food Crisis (1945–50)

When bananas were introduced to the British market after World War I, it marked the start of a love affair with this colourful fruit. Fruit was good for you, ran the message, and the quickly-unzipped, easy-to-bite banana seemed the ideal way to consume it.

In World War II, however, foodstuffs of all kinds were scarce and would become scarcer still as the Nazi blockade intensified. Emergency laws were passed to control what was eaten and the Ministry of Food was set up to act as enforcer. Ration books were introduced to control the consumption of meat, eggs, butter and sugar, and imported foodstuffs were kept to a minimum. Only one kind of fruit grown abroad was to be allowed, but would it be the orange or the banana? It would be the orange, decreed the Ministry, which then mounted an anti-banana propaganda campaign to suppress any unpatriotic longing. There were few vitamins in a banana, it lied, and its energy value was practically nil. Carrots and potatoes were better for you, and anyway, carrots enabled you to see in the dark (absolute rubbish but that's what They said), which was A Good Thing, as everything had to be blacked out in order to hinder German bombing raids. And so the banana was banished to live in folk memory as an exotic treasure of a bygone era, while the population tightened its collective belt, grew as much of its own food as possible and knuckled down to the war effort.

As crowds of cheering civilians and servicemen filled Britain's streets and squares when peace returned in May 1945, no one supposed then that rationing would not only continue but get very much more stringent. The return of Attlee's Labour government, promising a new beginning and 'fair shares for all', offered the prospect of a bright future after the years of self-sacrifice in the field, in the air, on the sea, under the Nazi bombs and in the deprived kitchens. The only trouble was that Britain was as near broke as makes little difference, and the new government had radical ideas to implement – industries to be nationalised wholesale and a new National Health Service to be set up – and if that meant putting the population on starvation rations, that's the way it would have to be – and was.

So, far from being abolished, the Ministry of Food swelled like a dropsical belly and, by the end of 1945, had 42,000 staff. Anything edible came under stringent control. Of some essentials, the weekly ration now stood at: sugar – one cup; eggs – one; bacon – four rashers; tea – 2oz; lard – one square.

Not surprisingly, the weary, already half-starved population was dismayed, so the government devised a colourful wheeze to make things seem, at least, less bad. It secretly imported 10 million bananas from Jamaica and sprang the surprise on New Year's Day 1946. As Geoff Spikins of the importing company Fyffes noted, 'It was a bright, cheery fruit. It made you feel better.' And, for a brief moment, it did. Growing kids who had only ever heard of this exotic fruit as a legend whispered in the playground now got a taste of it.

The event wasn't without its melodramatic moments. In a darkened Streatham cinema a young man secreted one in his pocket as a surprise for his girlfriend. He took her hand and guided it across his lap towards the desirable firm fruit. As her hand closed around it, her piercing scream caused the lights to go up and the film to be halted in mid-flicker.

This was not the only way the government's well-intentioned gesture went limp. Having stirred the nation's taste buds after six years of deprivation, it then found that the Jamaican farmers had sold all their stock and couldn't supply more than a trickle thereafter. The banana went back under state control, available only to pregnant women and young children.

1946 had not long dawned before the food ration was cut further. Dried egg was withdrawn and the weekly meat allowance fell to 5oz, with 2oz of corned beef to eke it out. By now, rebellion was in the air, and the newly formed Housewives' League forced the Food Ministry to withdraw its proposal to ration bread – a basic commodity that not even Hitler had succeeded in restricting.

As food supplies were further cut in 1947, defiance grew apace, so the Ministry began to employ spies in every town and openly encouraged the public to inform on each other. To the long-suffering population, it seemed as though the government was determined to deprive it not just of food but of every form of enjoyment as well. Indeed, in 1948, Britain was as close to a police state as it has ever been. As Mark Roodhouse of the University of York, commented, 'British society . . . was almost at breakdown. There was strong emphasis on enforcement, almost like a new Gestapo' – or, he might have said, a new NKVD, for this austere socialist government, determined that only it knew what was good for you, was demonstrating a brand of government perilously close to Stalinism, albeit without the executions.

In such a climate, black markets flourish, and a good few of those that sprang up in the late 1940s were operated by ex-servicemen fed up with the bleakness of life after their wartime efforts. The government sought to blacken them with the name 'spivs', but this, as any psychologist could have warned, had the immediate and opposite effect of making the spiv a glamorous figure helping people to exercise free choice at the expense of a grim bureaucracy.

By 1949, the UK crime rate had risen to unprecedented heights, and the Tories, mindful of forthcoming elections, launched the slogan 'The freedom to consume,' insisting that people must be allowed to buy their own home, their own car, their own holiday. The sentiment found favour and by 1951 they were back in power, promising – and delivering – a new age of prosperity. Labour complained that, without their age of austerity, there could have been no age of prosperity, and in fact they were at least half right. It had been the thankless and uncompromising way in which they'd gone about enforcing their restrictions on a population weary in mind and body that was their undoing and meant that, for the next thirteen years, they would have nothing but complaints to offer.

From 1950 onwards, step by step and year by year, rationing was lifted. Ironically, the banana was almost the last item to come off the list, in December 1952.

Battling Bessie Dances A Jig

Bessie Braddock Becomes The First Woman To Be Suspended By The Speaker Of The House (1947)

With vital statistics of 50–40–50, the wonderful Bessie Braddock wasn't a woman to be taken lightly. If, metaphorically speaking, the MP for Liverpool Exchange landed on you with full force, you were likely to need all of the long summer recess in which to recover. In her youth Bessie had, in her own words, 'joined the Communist Party because I was a rebel. I left it for the same reason. I was a rebel and I still am. The Communist Party hates social democracy even more than it hates Toryism.' That was Bessie in a nutshell, a woman who fought like a cornered animal for social justice but loved the democratic process of Westminster, and although there were those who would look for any means to attack her for her outspoken approach, there were others who – eventually – came to honour her for it.

In Bessie's maiden speech as an MP in 1945, she gave notice of the way in which she intended to continue by denouncing the 'bug-ridden, lice-ridden, rat-ridden, lousy hell holes' that were Liverpool's slums. And if her forthright language failed to gain the attention she sought for her beloved Liverpudlians, she had other methods at her disposal. In 1956, concerned about the proliferation of air rifles among the juveniles in her constituency, she marched into the Commons chamber toting three examples (they were, as it happened, unloaded, but only Bessie knew that at the time), which she raised in turn and fired before crossing the floor and depositing them in the lap of the Home Secretary. When the Deputy Speaker's nose cautiously rose over the edge of his desk to express his disapproval of such behaviour, Bessie replied, 'I have to startle this House before anyone does anything. No one takes any notice unless someone does something out of order or unusual.' She had a point.

The caper that got her into trouble happened much earlier in her career, during a debate on a transport bill in 1947. On that occasion, the opposition Tories registered their profound disagreement with those proposing the nationalisation of the rail services by deserting the chamber *en masse*, but several Labour MPs crossed the floor to sit on the opposition side of the House and thereby save the Transport Minister from having to address empty benches. This all seems perfectly blameless today, and wasn't exactly calculated to foreshadow the destruction of democracy even in its time, but the *Bolton Evening News* ran an article under the headline 'REVELRY AT NIGHT' in which it chose to interpret the act as a Braddock-inspired show of disrespect to Parliament. She had, it said, danced an 'Irish jig', an 'unlovely burlesque'.

Ridiculous? Of course it was. Utterly. But Bessie was greatly upset. Her devotion to the principles and practices of the Commons was already deeply entrenched, and the very idea that she might be thought to have shown a lack of respect for them appalled her. She brought a libel case against the publishers, and a special jury was empowered to hear it. Unfortunately – and you've probably guessed the outcome – that jury was a respectable, well-heeled, middle-class one, already well acquainted with the tales that the press so avidly reported of Bessie's outspoken tactics in the Commons on behalf of the seriously deprived working class of Liverpool. She lost her case and became the first female MP to be suspended by the Speaker of the House.

But, as her 25-year tenure as an MP progressed, Bessie's honesty and passion came to be recognised by opponents and colleagues alike. Although it was Churchill who, in response to Bessie's admonishing cry of 'Winston, you're drunk', delivered the famous riposte, 'Bessie, you are ugly, but tomorrow morning I shall be sober', it was also Churchill who became the first to acknowledge her abilities and her devotion to parliament by asking her to sit on the Royal Commission on Mental Health in 1954. In 1968, her own party honoured her by making her vice-chairman. She retired in 1970 and a year later she was dead, deeply mourned throughout Liverpool and much of the country.

By Gad, Sir, You're A Bounder!

Lt-Col Sir Walter Bromley-Davenport Causes A Diplomatic Incident (1951)

You may or may not be a fan of Neil Hamilton, with or without Christine in the van, but his knowledge of some of the great characters of the Commons, as detailed in his book *Great Political Eccentrics*, is never less than entertaining. Perhaps unsurprisingly, he has warm memories of a predecessor in his Tatton constituency rejoicing in the unequivocally Tory name of Sir Walter Bromley-Davenport who, having established the stereotype with his name, proceeded to live up to it with enthusiasm. As befitted a wartime colonel, Sir Walter's voice wasn't the least of his trademarks; described as stentorian, a bark uttered by him in Westminster might, with a following wind, have carried all the way to reach the ears of his Cheshire constituents.

As was often the case with those whose family tradition demanded that they devote their lives to disinterested (as they saw it) public service, Sir Walter wasn't especially concerned with holding high office, or indeed any office at all other than that of an MP. Three generations of his predecessors had been members of parliament, and although he could boast more distant ancestors who had held great offices of state under Queen Elizabeth I and Queen Anne, he saw no need for his latter-day family to covet their eminence. Nevertheless, his army training came in useful when he spent some time as an opposition whip between 1948 and

39

1951, and his fall from grace, when it came, was spectacular. Indeed, with a larger army at their disposal, the Belgians might well have declared war on us.

The 1950 general election saw the Labour Party return to power with a majority of eight, and it seemed clear to most observers that they could not long remain in power with such a precarious command over the House. The Conservatives therefore decided to put them on the rack with as many late-night sittings and snap votes as possible, and orders went out that all major debates were to be fully attended and voted on by the MPs, so the whips had to be especially vigilant to prevent anyone on their side from slipping off to a warm bed or a night on the town. Whenever a voting trap was to be sprung, a cry would go up: 'All doors', meaning that each whip had to man an exit from the Lobby.

On one such occasion, Sir Walter was standing guard outside the door to the Members' Entrance when what should he spy but a turncoat in a dinner jacket and bow tie sneaking rapidly across the Lobby. The Bromley-Davenport voice of command rose to full pitch as he ordered the escapee back to the ranks. Astonishingly, this weapon that usually had the power to stun the enemy in its tracks, produced no response. Sir Walter hastened to intercept the miscreant, whose face admittedly he didn't recognise (but then one Tory MP looked much like another to him), and was thrust aside.

Sir Walter had one weapon still at his disposal, and he deployed it forthwith. He gave the receding figure a firm boot up the backside and had the satisfaction of seeing it perform a none-too-graceful roll down the staircase to end up in a winded heap at the bottom.

Alas, it was not a Tory MP at all. It would have been some consolation if it had been, and preferably a Labour one or, better still, a member of the cabinet. It was none of these desirable targets; it was instead His Excellency the Belgian ambassador to the Court of St James, retiring to the safety of his embassy after an official function. There was, as they say, an incident, and Lt-Col Sir Walter Bromley-Davenport's brief flirtation with the perils of office was brought to an abrupt end. He was returned forthwith to the back benches, where he remained happily ensconced for a further nineteen years and where – as his *Guardian* obituary put it –

'nobody looked to him for quiet scrutiny, liberal thinking or deep and patient analysis, [but where he] gave a good deal of simple, if hardly quiet, pleasure'.

What Can Go Wrong Will Go Wrong

The 'Bay Of Pigs' Fiasco (Cuba, 1961)

President Fulgenci Batista of Cuba had been looking forward to 1959. It promised to be another comfortable year in the presidential palace, with Uncle Sam's big business boys running most of the country for him and those nice young men from the Mafia with bulges in all the right places making sure nobody complained about it. However, shortly after everyone in the palace had gone to bed in the small hours of New Year's Day to nurse their hangovers from the Hogmanay celebrations the previous night, who should come bursting in and upsetting it all but a chap called Fidel Castro with a big beard and a bunch of rowdies.

It was all too bad, and that nice President Eisenhower in the White House thought so too. In fact, Ike was seriously upset about it. Not only did he have to postpone his golf to take irate calls from businessmen demanding that he got their land and businesses back for them but, almost as bad, Cuba was only ninety miles from the American mainland. This Castro chappie was rumoured to be as thick as thieves with those awful Soviets in the Kremlin. If he wasn't careful, there'd be Russians swarming all over the place before you could say 'stars and stripes', converting bars and casinos into spy centres. He asked his vice-president, Richard 'Tricky Dickie' Nixon, to come up with a plan while he enjoyed eighteen nerve-soothing holes. By the time John F Kennedy had beaten Nixon in the 1960 presidential election, the plan was in place, and when he got seated in the Oval Office, Kennedy found that he quite liked it.

The plan was for 1,300 exiled Cubans to drop in unannounced, helped along by some disguised American planes, and, needing something to do while they were there, would quietly dispose of Castro. Naturally, the Cuban population would be on their side. Who could possibly want the iron hand of social reform in place of Mafia-run casinos and other places of relaxation where you could put your feet up and forget about the rigours of eking out a living for your family?

Even so, Kennedy was cautious. On no account could such righteous action be linked to the US of A. Perish the thought. It was imperative, in the jargon of the day, to ensure that there was no loss of deniability; as a secret memo to the president ran, 'When lies must be told, they should be told by subordinate officials.'

Accordingly, on the morning of 15 April 1961, three flights of Douglas Invaders displaying the markings of the Cuban Revolutionary Air Force took off from American bases to strafe Cuban airfields. They were preceded by one plane that had been shot up in advance of take-off, and its exiled pilot was to overfly Cuba, then radio a mayday call claiming that he'd been attacked over the island. He was to ask for clearance to land in Florida and then declare to the media that an uprising was taking place in his homeland, that defecting Cuban pilots were attacking airfields and that he had escaped to request asylum in the US.

On 17 April, the 1,300-plus exiles, armed with US weaponry, landed on the beaches fringing the Bay of Pigs on the southern coast of Cuba, anticipating an enthusiastic welcome. They got it, but not quite in the manner they had been anticipating. To their horror, it seemed that the local populace wasn't pining for a return to good old American values, as they'd assumed, but rather fancied the ideas that this Castro fellow was promoting. Worse still, the ground they now had to fight on was surrounded by marshes, making escape difficult. They were quickly surrounded and, after two days of fighting, nearly a hundred of the invaders were dead and 1,200 were on their way to thirty years in chokey. For the Americans, deniability had suddenly become a very tricky headache.

Being no fools, the first thing the Cubans did was complain to the United Nations' General Assembly in New York. Since (as it was to emerge many years later) the Russians had all along known about the plot and informed Cuba of the exact week in which it was to take place, the latter was primed and ready to deliver its complaint in the most public way possible. In response, however, the American ambassador to the UN, Adlai Stevenson, derided the charges and displayed photos of the Douglas Invaders with their fake Cuban markings.

As White House officials watched, they were overcome with shock and embarrassment. Nobody had bothered to tell Stevenson, an honourable man, what was really going on; he believed Washington's elaborate cover story to be true, and was predictably furious when the truth emerged 24 hours later. Even as the 1,300 exiles were beginning their forlorn battle in the marshes behind the Bay of Pigs, all hopes of US deniability had vanished and Kennedy very soon had to admit the White House's central role in the plot.

The passage of time made the fiasco even more embarrassing than it had first appeared. The CIA had been taking prior soundings of Cuban attitudes towards the Castro regime, but as one of their operatives, E Howard Hunt, reported, 'All I could find was a lot of enthusiasm for him.' The operation cost America $53 million in food and medicine as ransom for the 1,200 captured invaders, who felt little gratitude towards the US and felt – like many of the exiles now domiciled in Florida – that Kennedy could have saved the day for them if he'd sent in the Marines.

The ill-fated venture greatly deepened Castro's mistrust of his mighty neighbour and drove him further into the arms of the Soviet Union, who, convinced that America was in the hands of a weak and incompetent president, decided to convert Cuba into a missile base. Two years later, the consequent standoff between the two superpowers brought the world closer to nuclear war than ever before or since.

'Never Glad Confident Morning Again'

The Profumo Affair (1963)

1963 was a bad year for politics. In America, the hope and excitement engendered by John F Kennedy's fresh young presidency were abruptly terminated by a rifle shot in Dallas, Texas. In Britain a tired administration set in the ways of the past was shaken to its core, and ultimately its destruction, by a scandal that showed the establishment at its self-protecting worst as it lashed out at the minor players in an attempt to deflect odium onto others.

The story had simple and familiar beginnings. In 1961, John Profumo, the independently wealthy Secretary of State for War in Harold Macmillan's Conservative administration, became infatuated with an attractive nineteen-year-old girl named Christine Keeler. Like many before and since, Christine and another player in the story, Mandy Rice-Davies, had fled their tough working-class surroundings to seek work in showbusiness, and adventure in general, under the bright lights of London. Christine had a room in a flat owned by an osteopath named Stephen Ward, whose clients came mainly from distinguished social backgrounds.

Having encountered a naked Keeler in a swimming pool on the Cliveden estate of Lord Astor, Profumo pursued her relentlessly during the following months. Inevitably, since he was a minister of the Crown, their meetings were hurried, secret and to the point. Just as in Victorian times, it was considered acceptable within Westminster to have an affair as long as you didn't draw attention to it; as Labour MP Reginald Paget put it (albeit obliquely) when rumours of Profumo's activities were first raised in the House of Commons, 'A minister is said to be acquainted with an extremely pretty girl. As far as I am concerned, I should have thought that was a matter for congratulation rather than an inquiry.'

Had that been all there was to the story, such an attitude might well have prevailed, but what Profumo did not know was that, while she was seeing him regularly and hurriedly, Christine was enjoying herself much less hurriedly and to far greater effect in the arms of a handsome Soviet naval attaché, Colonel Eugene Ivanov. As she later told the *News of the World* (and it's anyone's guess who was the more breathless during these revelations, Christine or the reporter), 'I yielded to this wonderful huggy bear of a man . . . He was a wonderful lover, so masculine.'

This is precisely where the tale began to get murky. The Cold War was at its height and the Cuban missile crisis – when East and West came closer to war than at any time since World War II – was fresh in people's minds. Aware that Ivanov was visiting Keeler at Stephen Ward's flat but not yet that the Minister for War was a player in the drama, MI5 began to ponder the idea that Christine might be used to wring information from the Russian. Then Profumo's involvement came to MI5's ears and the idea was hurriedly dropped. The question was, what kind of pillow talk were Keeler, Profumo and Ivanov engaged in? And, if there was any, who was saying what to whom? Discreet warnings were passed to the minister via the Cabinet Secretary, but despite them he went on seeing Keeler until December 1961, when the relationship ended.

There followed a year in which all fell quiet on the Profumo–Keeler front. She continued to live in Stephen Ward's flat, where she was joined by Mandy Rice-Davies (or Mandy Rice-Pudding, as wags would call her once she achieved notoriety). The former had a couple of West Indian lovers on the go, and Mandy had a brief affair with a man named Peter Rachman, who was already attracting tabloid attention for his ruthless exploits as a slum landlord. These characters were further ingredients in the explosive mixture being readied for detonation under the apparently peaceful surface of 1962.

The shot that opened the fateful campaign was the first of several fired at the front door of Ward's flat when Christine refused entry to one of her West Indian lovers. The police moved in with a charge of attempted murder, press reporters began sniffing about and, with money as the eternal inducement, Keeler began to talk to them. Even so, the press were cautious and for three months a kind of phoney war existed as rumours swept the country – or, at any rate, the Commons, which, as far as MPs were concerned, amounted to the same thing. The Prime Minister was alerted and issued a response, saying, 'Profumo has behaved foolishly and indiscreetly, but not wickedly. His wife is very nice and sensible.' He did nothing.

Over on the opposition benches was one George Wigg – possibly as self-centred and ruthless an MP as ever sat in the Commons. Hearing the rumours he had begun compiling a dossier on Profumo (against whom he held a personal grudge). He saw the chance to launch a torpedo at him in the shape of a demand that a Select Committee be formed to investigate rumours concerning an unnamed minister. The following day, Profumo made a long statement to his fellow MPs in which he mentioned Ivanov but flatly and categorically denied that he'd had an affair with Christine Keeler.

By now, though, the fat was well and truly in the fire, and Profumo's mention of Ivanov allowed the press to connect his rumoured affair with security. Meanwhile, George Wigg – reckless of lesser people's reputations – began to denounce Stephen Ward as a security risk, for which there was then, nor has there ever been any evidence.

As ever, the establishment tried to close ranks and silence the fringe players by subjecting them to police pressure. Mandy Rice-Davies was imprisoned for a few days in an attempt to soften her up and persuade her to implicate Ward, who was already being investigated and, as a result, losing his socialite friends. The tactic worked to the extent that, in order to save himself, Ward wrote letters in which he denounced Profumo for lying about his affair with Keeler. It was enough for the Minister for War to be compelled to return from his holiday, confess that he had lied to the House and resign. He slipped away to Ireland with his family and devoted the rest of his life to charity work.

The press, suddenly brave with the danger of being sued for libel out of the way, now called open season on those who remained. The rumour mill went into overdrive and no whiff of uninvestigated scandal was too slight to make the front pages, no matter how innocent or naïve the people that were hurt as a result. In the course of the hysteria, Christine Keeler was jailed for six months for contempt of court and, after a trial that was little better than a travesty, Stephen Ward committed suicide. One of the two wreaths at his funeral, from a group of distinguished playwrights and actors, read, 'VICTIM OF HYPOCRISY'. (It was no accident that Arthur Miller's play *The Crucible*, about the persecution of the so-called Witches of Salem and originally written as a reaction against the McCarthyite denunciations of alleged communists in 1950s America, found itself being revived in 1960s Britain at this time.) Only Mandy Rice-Davies managed to bounce through the sordid repercussions with a degree of dignity and humour. Asked at Ward's trial why Lord Astor now denied knowing her, she replied, 'Well, he would, wouldn't he?', a riposte that perfectly summed up the way in which the establishment pretended not to know those it had been exploiting all along. There was one other small but cheering footnote: the appalling and self-righteous George Wigg was later caught and prosecuted for kerb-crawling.

In the aftermath of the affair, MP Nigel Birch quoted Browning in the House when he said it would 'never [be] glad confident morning again'. Indeed, it could be argued that our current indifference to our politicians dates back to 1963 and that the supposedly 'swinging sixties' were an ostentatious shrug of the nation's shoulders as it determined to follow its own values and instincts rather than those of its unreliable leaders.

Wilson Devalues His Credibility

The Pound Plummets (1967)

The trouble with politicians – or, at least, most of those who achieve office and power – is that they assume the electorate to have a mental age of eleven. This is not a new phenomenon but a permanent political condition. No matter how often elections or referenda demonstrate the almost instinctive grasp of essential issues possessed by the voters, nothing seems to shake the politicians' belief that only they understand what's going on. Harold Wilson proved to be no exception to this rule.

In 1967, as summer turned to autumn, speculation became increasingly feverish about the value of the pound, which in those days was fixed at US $2.80, a level that seemed far too generous to the pound. The problem that Wilson's Labour government had to wrestle with was that large parts of the Commonwealth kept their reserves in the Bank of England, and a devaluation of sterling would automatically write down those reserves with all the dangers of lost confidence in the City of London. If sterling lost its standing as a hard currency, there was every likelihood that gold from South Africa and Australia and other precious metals, not to mention valuable commodity trades such as wool from Down Under, would seek a home away from Britain.

On the other hand, the post-World War II economic miracle in Germany was still in full swing. There, the banks were sitting on mountainous cash surpluses, allowing low interest rates and, in consequence, the most favourable export prices for their cars and engineering equipment.

In comparison, the demand for British goods declined as their prices rose, egged upwards by an artificially high pound. The balance-of-payments deficit rose and went on rising. The World Bank got edgy and began to apply increasing pressure on Britain to devalue its currency, a solution that threatened to upset the world's trade, given sterling's status as an important trading currency.

The only way out of the dilemma seemed to be for Germany to *up*value the mark. If this could not be achieved, then Britain had either to borrow heavily from overseas banks or face up to devaluation. There. That was all quite simple, wasn't it? Why couldn't Harold have told it as it really was?

Instead, he hauled the German ambassador out of bed in the early hours of 20 November and summoned him to Downing Street. That, at any rate is how the tabloids triumphantly presented it, as though the sight of a German in pyjamas somehow signalled moral disintegration. In fact, Herr Blankenhorn had been expecting Wilson's call and was fully dressed for his confrontation. He promised to convey the British government's views to Bonn immediately, but although the Germans did revalue the mark, they didn't do so by enough to save the British pound. The Bank of England had already poured £200 million worth of its gold and dollar reserves into its attempt to prop up the ailing currency and a stop had to be called. Accordingly, Harold Wilson announced a fourteen per cent cut in the value of the pound, bringing it down to US $2.40.

The prime minister now had to broadcast the news to the nation, and so, adopting his most smoothly reasonable and avuncular tone, he made the fateful announcement, 'From now, the pound abroad is worth fourteen per cent less in terms of other currencies. It does not mean,' he continued, warming to his theme, 'that the pound here in Britain, in your pocket or purse or in your bank, has been devalued.'

The populace gazed at their black and white television screens in bemusement. Those listening on the radio scratched their heads disbelievingly. Had our glorious leader not heard of Volkswagens and Mercedes imported from Germany, or Renaults and Peugeots from

France? Was he not aware that over fifty per cent of our foodstuffs came from abroad? And, since the problem was cheaper foreign goods than those we produced, did he suppose we were not buying them ourselves? If they were now to cost fourteen per cent more, how come the pound in our pockets was worth the same?

As soon as they'd got their breath back, satirists, cartoonists and impressionists leapt into action, lampooning the absurdity of the assertion. Debates in the Commons and the Lords turned the air blue with sarcasm. Deputy Prime Minister George Brown told his leader what he thought of him (in private, of course) and the Chancellor, 'Sunny' Jim Callaghan, who had opposed the devaluation in Cabinet meetings, resigned 'on a point of honour', a phrase that will be unfamiliar to younger readers but is the kind of thing politicians once used to do.

The whole point of the devaluation, Mr Wilson said, was to tackle the root cause of Britain's economic problems and to break away from the old patterns of 'boom and bust'. It did nothing of the kind, and when he went to the polls in 1970 on a platform of improved economic performance, he was defeated by Ted Heath and the Conservatives.

'He Would Get Drunk On The Smell Of The Cork'

George Brown Resigns On His Eighteenth Attempt (1968)

I don't wish to denigrate the name Brown. There are undoubtedly many wonderful and colourful people named Brown. Richmal Crompton's William Brown of *Just William* fame, for example, would undoubtedly have grown up – once the author had allowed him to progress beyond the age of nine – to be an intrepid explorer or a Battle of Britain ace. It's just that Brown, politics and the title 'second in command' seem to spell trouble, at least for the prime minister of the moment. Today it's the political tag team of Tony Blair and Gordon Brown who stalk each other through the long grass of Westminster. In the 1960s PM Harold Wilson had George Brown and spent most of his first term as premier, from 1964 to 1970, wishing he hadn't.

Ostensibly, the trouble arose when, following Hugh Gaitskell's unexpected death in 1962, Wilson was elected leader of the Labour Party, a position George Brown felt should rightfully have been his by dint of his background and intellectual capacity. He had, after all, been Gaitskell's deputy and commanded a trade-union power base, while Wilson was a left-wing intellectual, a wartime civil servant and an opportunist with few real principles who could have been in any party. He was, in short, the Blair of his day, while George Brown was a passionate social reformer and, by nature, confrontational – rather like a mix of namesake Gordon with, heaven help us, John Prescott. George was not pleased when he lost the 1962 Labour Party leadership vote. No sooner was the result announced than, to the delight of the party, Wilson called for George to be deputy leader, but Brown's response was to tilt his nose in the air and stalk off the platform. Although he accepted the post the following day, he made no secret thereafter of his contempt for 'the little man', as he referred to Wilson.

This was the prelude to four stormy years in which George saw insults lurking in every comment and every failure to consult him about matters in advance. Cabinet colleagues who had begun by being sympathetic to his plight gradually began to lose patience. 'He treated Harold absolutely abominably,' said Barbara Castle, never one to be found lacking for a forthright comment. 'He was a thorn in Harold's side . . . and didn't hide the fact that he thought he ought to have been leader. And he was a menace,' she added, 'partly because of his uncontrolled public behaviour.'

There, indeed, was the rub. It wasn't that George drank a lot but that, genetically speaking, as his teetotal brother Ron explained, alcohol and the Brown family simply didn't mix. 'He was one of those people who would get drunk on the smell of the cork,' said Castle. Another colleague, Defence Secretary Denis Healey, found that he had to schedule his weekly meetings with Brown before 12 noon, 'because otherwise there was the risk that George would be the worse for drink'.

Alcohol and paranoia make for a heady mix, and before long George's penchant for spotting insults where none had necessarily existed led to his resignations – and there were plenty of them. In July 1966, for example, George resigned (again) in protest at a wage freeze that was being mooted by the government, but a few hours later, around midnight, he was to be found on the steps of 10 Downing Street announcing to anyone who happened to be passing that he'd changed his mind. On another occasion, he phoned Wilson at 11 p.m. one night to announce that he'd had a row with his wife and would have to resign. His vacillation became reminiscent of the Parisian joke of the late 1940s and early 1950s as successive governments of the fourth republic fell after a few weeks in office, when

Parisians would chortle, 'I'm just popping down to the Elysée Palace to watch the changing of the government.'

Back in London, fifteen or so years later, Brown's resignations became so routine that Westminster wags tried to convince their more credulous colleagues that an aide had one day burst into Harold Wilson's office to tell him a resignation letter had just been received from the deputy premier. 'Just put it on the pile with all the others,' Harold was said to have answered.

On the occasion of George's sixteenth resignation – this time on a matter of foreign policy – he had stormed out of Wilson's office but returned later to carry on the argument. 'Now that the sixteenth resignation is out of the way,' Harold told him, 'we can discuss the matter further until the occasion comes for the seventeenth.'

By March 1968, however, Wilson had had enough. He and Chancellor Jim Callaghan were facing yet another economic crisis – this time a result of an emergency in the international gold market – and decided a bank holiday would have to be declared in order to prevent the banks from opening and precipitating a run on the pound. George was not told, but when he heard about it on the grapevine he went into his well-practised foot-stamping, top-blowing routine and phoned Downing Street, demanding to be put through to the PM. He had already gone to Buckingham Palace to inform the queen, but his Permanent Secretary told him that Downing Street had been trying to get hold of him all day. George decided to check the truth of this with the man in charge of the switchboard there, who told him that no call had been attempted that morning. In went resignation letter number eighteen, and this time no emollient response was forthcoming. George found himself making the short journey to the back benches and he lost his seat in the general election held two years later, won by Ted Heath and the Conservatives.

George On The Loose

The Foreign Secretary Endangers Diplomatic Relations With Uruguay (1967)

It's asking too much to tear oneself away from the subject of George Brown without delighting in his unfortunate if mercifully short-lived affair with the Cardinal Archbishop of Montevideo. As Barbara Castle said, 'The whole government was in danger when George was on the loose.'

In August 1966, George was translated from the Department for Economic Affairs to the Foreign Office. Presumably it was reckoned that whatever he got up to outside Britain would be interpreted as a triumph by the press at home, especially if it involved insulting General de Gaulle, who at the time was proving sticky about Britain's accession to the EEC.

George got off to a good start in his new job. As custom dictated, the entire staff of the majestic FO collectively put on its best bib and tucker and assembled in serried ranks in the awe-inspiring reception hall to greet the new master diplomat, the face of Britain abroad. They waited and waited, shuffling feet and clearing throats, but the new foreign secretary was nowhere to be seen. Surely he couldn't be still in bed after another bender the night before?

The mystery was solved by George's Principal Private Secretary, who, recalling some papers he needed, slipped upstairs and found George in his shirtsleeves behind his desk. Unaware of the tradition, he'd come in via a back door and had to be persuaded to go out the way he'd come and re-enter in splendour via the portals at the front of the building.

In his 21-month tenure at the Foreign Office, George remained true to form and contrived to insult almost everyone with whom he came into contact. His masterstroke was achieved early in his career at the FO during a state banquet in Montevideo, held to express the Uruguayans' thanks for Britain's support in their long-distant struggle for independence from Spain. On that occasion, the natives had turned out *en masse* in their most glittering South American uniforms and Paris-inspired gowns. The staff of the British Embassy had briefed George extensively on the protocol expected of him, and he managed to remember that, after the banquet, toasts would be drunk, the band would strike up and he would be expected to lead the Uruguayan president's wife onto the dance floor.

George decided that this was the kind of evening he would enjoy, and so he did. Champagne preceded a selection of excellent wines, and the food and drink slipped effortlessly down the Foreign Secretary's throat before he addressed himself to the port. So far, so good; he'd got a considerable way through the evening without insulting anybody or getting engaged in an argument. The chaps in the Embassy – whose names, admittedly, he couldn't for the life of him remember – would be very pleased with him.

At this point, the band sprang into life, and George forgot all about the toasts. If the band was playing, that meant it was time to dance, and if it was time to dance, it was time to find the president's wife. He was sure he must have spoken to her earlier on, but he was dashed if he could remember what she looked like. Ah! There she was, in a beautiful red silk dress. George leapt – or, rather, stumbled – to his feet, made for the dress standing to attention on the other side of the table, seized it by its resisting arm and hauled it onto the dance floor.

The next morning, after his head had cleared, it was explained to him where he'd made a slight error of judgement. What the band had struck up with was the Uruguayan national anthem, and the owner of the beautiful silk red dress had been His Eminence the Cardinal Archbishop of Montevideo, who, like Queen Victoria before him, had remained obstinately unamused. Fortunately for George and, more particularly, for the Uruguayans, his stay at the Foreign Office proved to be too brief to allow a return visit.

Enoch In Deep Waters

Enoch Powell Foresees 'Rivers Of Blood' (1968)

When Enoch Powell died in 1998, politicians of the day praised him as being a great patriot, parliamentarian and practitioner of conviction politics but carefully avoided all mention of immigration. This was an issue too close to contemporary concerns (albeit in greatly altered circumstances) to risk reminding anyone of how Powell had set the nation in uproar with his notorious 'rivers of blood' speech in 1968.

A word much-favoured by those trying to describe Enoch Powell's character is 'enigmatic', although a more accurate one might be 'contradictory'. In some respects he was a politician of the hard right, yet in others a thoughtful social reformer. Of only one thing, perhaps, could one be certain: he mistrusted orthodoxy and was liable to oppose the current view on any matter of the moment.

Powell was a man of achievement in many fields – scholarship, philosophy, poetry, soldiering and oratory – who settled into politics as his chosen preoccupation. One might expect that this breadth of experience would make him a man able to see and occupy the middle ground, but, as Norman Shrapnel wrote in his obituary of him, Powell 'had little time for the reasonable man's halfway house where most tolerable life is carried on'.

As the United Kingdom withdrew from its imperial past in the fifteen to twenty years after World War II and inhabitants of former colonies exercised their right to come and live in Britain, racial tensions began to ferment. No host-country, however well-intentioned, can struggle with the sweeping social changes at work in 1950 and 1960s Britain without the risk of occasional outbursts of serious, if localised, violence, and this is exactly what happened most notably in the Notting Hill riots of 1958.

Trouble continued to simmer in the 1960s, and Birmingham's Smethwick district was regarded as an incipient problem area. Powell was the MP for a nearby constituency, Wolverhampton Southwest, when he chose – without prior warning to any in his party – to go on the offensive in a speech to the West Midlands Conservative Party. It would be melodramatic to say that what he said on the evening of 20 April 1968 was the equivalent of throwing a match into a barrel of gunpowder, were it not for the fact that Powell himself acknowledged that very thing in his speech. Indeed, in the immediate aftermath, many feared he'd done exactly that.

Powell's intended objective might have been to force people to confront the immigration policy (or lack thereof) of the day. There was, he was convinced, a conspiracy of silence cloaking a refusal to think through the long-term consequences for jobs, housing, health, transport infrastructure – and community relations. 'In fifteen to twenty years, on present trends,' he predicted, 'there will be in this country 3,500,000 Commonwealth immigrants and their descendants. That is the official figure given to parliament by the Registrar General's office.' By the year 2000, he continued, that number would be between 5 million and 7 million. 'Can it be limited,' he asked, 'bearing in mind that numbers are of the essence?' Such a question was in itself reasonable enough. What provoked uproar was the language he used and the 'men in the street' he quoted to make points that went far beyond questions of demographics and their economic consequences, and which gave the impression of a racist attitude.

This is precisely where Powell's inability to take up the central position 'where most tolerable life is carried on' was his undoing. Whether he intended to go as far as he did, or whether he was intoxicated by his own oratory, we may never know. What he did was to quote a 'quite ordinary' working man as saying, among other things, that in 'fifteen or twenty years' time, the black man will have the whip hand over the white man'. This led him on to make his most widely-quoted and widely-reviled quotation, this time from the Roman poet Virgil: 'I am filled with foreboding. I seem to see the River Tiber foaming with much blood.'

Very little imagination is required to visualise the furore that this created. In a single speech, Powell had become the mouthpiece for a sizeable section of the population that was confused, frightened and, therefore, intolerant. When Ted Heath immediately responded to the speech by sacking Powell from the Shadow Cabinet (he was never to hold office again), 2,000 London dockers walked off the job. Protest marchers converged on the Commons in support of Powell and further industrial protests were organised. The 'quite ordinary' working man, it seemed, was real enough. However, there was an even greater proportion of the population that wanted nothing to do with such attitudes, and they too made their anger felt in public meetings and demonstrations.

It is almost beyond question that Enoch Powell's 'rivers of blood' speech was the biggest clanger dropped in domestic politics in half a century, but it left an unanswerable question: did it, ultimately, do UK citizens a service by forcing them to confront attitudes that had been buried too long beneath the surface and, thereby, to begin the long process of cleansing them?

Shortly after Powell's speech, a Methodist chaplain named WW Alphonse gave his vision of the future, which, far from being one of 'the Tiber foaming with blood', was rather one of clean, fresh water made up of the many tributaries of mankind – or, as Churchill put it (albeit in a different context), 'A genius springs from every class and from every part of the land. You cannot tell where you will not find a wonder. The hero, the fighter, the master of science, the organiser, the engineer, the administrator or the jurist – he may spring into fame. Equal opportunity from free institutions and equal laws.'

'You Have Just Been Hit By Spiro Agnew'

US Vice-President Forced To Resign (1973)

On being made vice-president of the United States by Richard Nixon in 1971, Spiro T Agnew whiled away his idle hours – vice-presidents have little purpose in life other than hanging about in case the President drops dead – by discovering a passion for golf. He wasn't very good at the game, and it was wise to be 250 or more yards away from him – in any direction, including to the rear – when he was, so to speak, on strike. At the annual Bob Hope Desert Classic at Palm Springs one year he nailed three unwary spectators with his first two shots. Thereafter, it was said that he had the words 'You have just been hit by Spiro Agnew' inscribed on the golf balls he distributed with abandon on either side of the fairways. It was not with golf balls alone, however, that he carried out his remorseless strikes on the public.

Politics is a devious occupation at the best of times, but in the early 1970s in America it was about as dodgy as it gets, as we shall see in the very next section. Those who had crossed Nixon's path before knew that he wasn't the most gentlemanly of opponents and that he didn't fight the straightest of fights, so it should have been little surprise when he offered the vice-presidency to an ex-lawyer of doubtful repute who had gone on to become governor of Maryland, a state little bigger than its main city, Baltimore, and barely registering on the consciousness of most Americans. As one cynic put it, the highlight of Agnew's record was his introduction of programmes to assist needy governors of Maryland named Agnew. Deep suspicion surrounded the kickbacks he was said to have taken from major contractors, and the mysterious way in which campaign contributions were forever turning up in small-denomination notes stuffed into brown envelopes. So frequently did the governor discover little brown envelopes in his pockets as he disrobed for bed that in no time he was able to mount an election campaign costing at least $200,000.

Once safely appointed vice-president, Spiro's instructions were pretty much to set about all pinkos, lefties and weirdos (the last being a generic term for the first two, along with Democrats). As his written efforts were a tad lacking in style (and apparently the spelling wasn't too hot either), he hired a couple of scriptwriters. One of his favourite speeches could be applied to any enemy he took a fancy to attacking (although it was most frequently directed at reporters and intellectuals) and ran, 'The media/intellectuals/lefties/pinkos/Democrats (delete as applicable) are an effete corps of impudent snobs, a tiny fraternity of privileged people elected by no one and enjoying a monopoly sanctioned and licensed by the government. They are nattering nabobs of negativism.'

This was, of course, guaranteed to win him the implacable opposition of almost every journalist in the land, but he was only just getting started. When he declared, 'A Nixon–Agnew administration will abolish the credibility gap and re-establish the truth – the whole truth – as its policy,' they knew exactly what he meant: the left wing and centre press would be ruthlessly targeted, and any questions about unethical behaviour on his or Nixon's part would be suppressed.

What neither Nixon nor Agnew had foreseen was that Tricky Dickie's nefarious shenanigans at the Watergate Hotel in Washington, DC, during the president's 1971 re-election campaign would come to public light. The first questions began to be asked in 1972, soon after his inauguration, and as the months passed suspicions of dishonesty and corruption in the administration grew ever greater. It was only to be expected that, having made himself so pleasant to the gentlemen of the press, Spiro T's dubious acquisition of little brown envelopes stuffed with greenbacks would join the accusations being thrown at the White House. 'Damned lies,' thundered Spiro, and vowed never to step down from the vice-presidency. Over the next few months, however, this avowal became a little like a chorus from Gilbert and Sullivan's *HMS Pinafore.* 'Never?' 'No, never!' 'What, never?' 'Well, almost never.'

On 10 October 1973, Agnew was forced to resign, knowing that within hours he would be served with a court order requiring him to answer charges of tax evasion. He was convicted, fined and debarred from practising law in Maryland. After appeals and nine years of wrangling, in 1983 he was finally required to pay back to the State of Maryland the amount of the bribes it was proved he had received, totalling $268,482.

There but for the grace of God and the courts of Maryland went the next US president. Gerald Ford was appointed VP in Agnew's place, and when Nixon also resigned from office, in 1974, it was Ford, not Spiro T Agnew, who became the 38th President of the United States.

'There Will Be No Whitewash At The White House'

Richard M Nixon And The Watergate Affair (1974)

Richard Milhous Nixon, 37th president of the United States, was not an easy man to like. To start with, he looked shifty, with a perennial five-o'clock shadow and untrustworthy eyes. 'Would you buy a second-hand car from this man?', his enemies asked, and the answer was generally a resounding NO. A man cannot help how he looks, but as television began to play an ever-more-important part in substituting image for substance, it was a handicap.

To many people, however, what was worse was where he stood in the political spectrum, and that was well to the right. He added to this a self-pitying streak that convinced him that his enemies (and that included anyone standing on the centre ground, never mind those to the left of it) were out to get him by any means possible. Thus, as his first presidential term drew to its close, he busied himself with raising funds for his re-election. The Committee to Re-elect the President (CRP) was formed, and its concerns were not limited to fund-raising alone; it applied its collective brains to finding ways of smearing and spying on the opposition.

On the night of 17 June 1972, the CRP despatched five burglars to break into the offices of the Democratic National Committee in the

Watergate Hotel in central Washington. The alarm was raised and the five were arrested, along with two of the planners, Gordon Liddy and Howard Hunt. In September of that year, all five were tried and convicted of burglary, conspiracy and wire-tapping. So far, so straightforward.

However, the question debated over morning coffee, brown-bag lunches and evening dinner tables was, did the President know? The murk descended, and for the next two years the national sport became that of peering ever deeper into the muddy waters in an effort to get to the truth.

John J Sirica, the judge who had presided over the trial of the burglars, was convinced that the truth was being carefully concealed and offered leniency in return for information. It became clear that the burglars had been in league with the CRP and the CIA (Criminal Investigation Agency), which appeared to have changed roles and become the CID (Criminal Instigation Department).

As Sirica probed, some of Nixon's aides began to talk. Jeb Magruder, assistant to CRP director John Mitchell, was one of the first defectors to feel the hot breath of conscience, and by early 1973 it was becoming clear that, if not the president himself, at least those in his inner circle were implicated. The Senate set up an investigative committee under the tough and fearless Senator Sam Ervin and featuring none other than Judge Sirica.

From then on, it was like peeling off the layers of a putrid onion one by one, and with each layer the White House core grew closer. As he ducked and weaved, Nixon began to dismiss those on whom, it was hoped, the blame might come to rest.

Soon the sky above Washington seemed black with the bodies of human cannonballs fired from their posts. John Ehrlichman and HR Haldeman, two of Nixon's apparently untouchable heavyweights, were required to lower themselves into the barrel. Then, barely had the whiff of cordite dissipated than John W Dean, his counsel, followed them. Two intrepid reporters at the *Washington Post*, Robert Woodward and Carl Bernstein, made contact with a mysterious informer from the higher reaches of the White House whose identity remained hidden under the code name 'Deep Throat' (now known to be former FBI associate director Mark Felt). As each layer of the onion was peeled away, the *Post* seemed to know exactly which question should be asked next. Each revelation merely roused the Senate investigative committee to new bursts of energy and it wasn't long before John W Dean was singing merrily, confirming that Nixon had indeed known of and approved a cover-up.

The next breakthrough came from Haldeman aide Alexander Butterfield, who informed the committee's special prosecutor, Archibald Cox, that Nixon had secretly tape-recorded conversations in the Oval office. The committee demanded the tapes, but the president cited 'executive privilege' and refused. More firings took place; more human cannonballs shot across town.

In March 1974, a federal grand jury indicted seven of President Nixon's closest aides, including John Mitchell, director of the CRP, and in parallel the House Judiciary Committee began investigating the whole Watergate scandal. The net was starting to close around Nixon, but his instinct to struggle and escape its clutches was strong. He agreed to supply some of the Oval office tapes, but these proved to have suspicious pauses at opportune moments, suggesting they had been edited. Sirica subpoenaed more tapes and was refused them.

Nixon tried one last throw of the dice and went on television to talk to the nation. Over twenty years earlier, when he'd been vice-president in Eisenhower's administration, he'd made a similar move to win over the support of the public against charges of accepting money illegally for campaign purposes. On that occasion he'd pulled a tear-jerker by producing the family dog, Checkers, and bluffed his way through, but Checkers had long since died. This time, Nixon settled for looking straight at the camera with what he hoped was an expression indicating candour and honesty while saying, with lamentable timing and intonation, 'There will be no whitewash at the White House.' His attempt to win over the nation failed, if for no other reason than it was already plain that there had been, if not a whitewash, an almighty cover-up.

In late July 1974, the House Judiciary Committee recommended the impeachment of Richard M Nixon. One week later, the president handed over three more tapes that revealed he had indeed tried to obstruct the investigation of the Watergate burglary and that he had been involved in the cover-up from the beginning. On 9 August 1974, he became the first – and, so far, only – president of the United States to resign from the position.

Who's In Charge Around Here?

Ted Heath Finds Out Who Runs Britain (1974)

You wouldn't need to be at the slipper'd and pantaloon'd stage to remember the miserable 1970s, although you would be watching your fortieth year disappear in your slipstream. The 1960s hadn't seen Britain at its brilliant best, although we were told later we had been 'swinging', and it's true that models like Jean 'the Shrimp' Shrimpton, groups like The Beatles and designers like Mary Quant had brightened the scene and allowed us to forget the country's miserable economic situation.

The next decade, offered no such luck. Then it was all flared trousers, long sideburns and daft haircuts. For entertainment there were hardline union bosses like Hugh Scanlon and Jack Jones, not to mention the yapping of a Yorkshire terrier named Arthur Scargill, although in truth there was little to laugh at in their increasingly preposterous demands.

Within six months of Tory Ted Heath's victory over Labour's Harold Wilson in the 1970 general election, strikes by dockers and power workers not only reduced the nation's stock of candles to dangerous levels but also prompted a state of emergency to be declared on two separate occasions. It was a foretaste of the industrial chaos to come through the rest of the decade.

As inflation rose steadily, ultimately to double figures, Heath strove to rein in wage increases that were often running at fifteen per cent a year. Having failed to win union co-operation, a ninety-day freeze was put on all wages, salaries and dividends in November 1972, followed six months later by a limit of £4 or one per cent and then, in October 1973, by a maximum of £2.25 or seven per cent, up to a ceiling of £350 for the year. While he was struggling to keep the lid on union demands, however, the price of imported raw materials had doubled, and in October 1973 the latest Arab–Israeli war saw the price of oil – the alternative fuel to coal – quadruple.

In such circumstances, a moderate union might have played its hand carefully, winning concessions for its members but understanding the limits beyond which even a weak government could not be pushed. However, although Joe Gormley, head of the NUM (National Union of Miners), was a moderate who was also a shrewd old bird and a master tactician, he in turn was under pressure. Neither Yorkshire's Arthur Scargill nor Scotland's Mick McGahey (who specialised in making his pronouncements utterly incomprehensible) had ever heard the word 'moderate', and were certainly not disposed to look it up. Although Heath was willing to break his own wage limits and concede sixteen per cent, it wasn't enough for Scargill and McGahey, who wanted control of the NUM. A strike was looming and the government announced the three-day week, determined to be prepared and not see coal stocks run out at the power stations in the middle of winter (and winters in those days meant snow and ice, often in considerable quantity). Signs reading 'SOS' ('Switch Off Something') were to be seen in windows and workplaces up and down the country as power rationing was introduced. There was an intangible sense that society was breaking down.

As stalemate threatened, Heath was persuaded, against his will, to call an election on 28 February 1974 in order to answer the question, who runs the country? The unions or the government? The answer, when it came, was the unions. Although the Tories shaded the popular vote by 300,000, they ceded a majority of four seats to Labour. The feeling seemed to be that Harold Wilson and the Labour Party had a better chance of persuading the NUM, and the unions in general, to see reason. If so, it was a vain hope; the national debt stood at £4 billion, yet the miners enforced a settlement of thirty-five per cent.

Two years later, Britain would suffer the ultimate humiliation of going cap in hand to the International Monetary Fund – usually accustomed to helping third-world countries – to be bailed out and put back on its shaky legs. The measures enforced as a result led to the infamous 'winter of discontent' and the appalling sight of uncollected garbage heaped in the streets and unburied bodies heaped in the mortuaries.

In the meantime, the Tories ditched Ted Heath pretty smartly and surprised itself with its own daring in voting for a woman – known to later generations as 'the Iron Lady' – to lead them. Mrs Thatcher had unfinished business with the NUM, but she bided her time while more and more power stations converted to oil. Gormley could see what was coming and retired in 1982, allowing Scargill to claim, as noisily as ever, his heart's desire as he became leader of the union and, he expected, a political force in the land.

By 1984, Mrs Thatcher was ready for him. The Coal Board announced the closure of twenty coal mines, Scargill snatched the bait like a shark smelling blood in the water and called an all-out strike in March 1984. It took a year, and much bitterness, to settle matters, but when the coal dust settled the NUM was broken and faded into obscurity.

Many years later, it emerged that Joe Gormley had warned MI5 of what was going on in the NUM. He was, said an MI5 member, 'a patriot, and he was very wary and worried about the growth of militancy within his own union.' After Gormley retired he was made a life peer, which half suggests there was truth to his allegation.

That apart, there's a certain irony that the man in charge of the NUM when it inflicted its most humiliating defeat on the government of the day should be so honoured. If the establishment was going to hand out such rewards, one would have expected one to be pinned on Arthur Scargill for so effectively wrecking the union by his lack of judgement and tactical nous.

Jonathan Confronts His Maker

A Spot Of Local Difficulty For Jonathan Aitken (1975)

It's commonly known that former cabinet minister Jonathan Aitken found God while doing a spot of chokey for telling porkies about his dealings with those nice men from Saudi Arabia (see the section titled 'I Am A Man Of Unclean Lips', pp. 120–123). His spell behind bars was brought about when he chose to confront the *Guardian* newspaper over the matter of his probity in this respect, whereupon he found to his horror that they had gathered together divers omens, artefacts and sayings inadvertently dropped by him in Paris. Having lost his honour and his career, not to mention a spell of freedom, what else could he do but seek enlightenment? Yet, twenty-odd years earlier, he'd had a brush with a figure of such omnipotence that one would have thought he'd have learned all about the Day of Judgement.

Back in 1975, Aitken had been a young, handsome member of the aristocracy (the aristocracy of the fourth estate, that is), being directly descended from Lord Beaverbrook, owner of the *Daily Express*. For some time, his girlfriend-in-chief had been Carol Thatcher, whose mother, by one of those happy and disarming accidents, was known to be involved in the very political party to which Mr Aitken belonged.

In that same year, Jonathan paid a visit to Saudi Arabia (where else?), where he was closeted with sundry members of that country's rather large ruling family. On emerging from one of these frank and friendly discussions, he was confronted by a reporter from the local English-language newspaper – not an organ of massive circulation and vast hitting power, as one might well imagine. What were his views, he was asked, on the candidates in the Tory leadership contest then taking place back in dear old Blighty? With Saudi Arabia being a very male-dominated society, the reporter wanted especially to hear a few thoughts on the prospects of his girlfriend's mother, who it seemed had tossed her handbag into the ring. Did she, for example, have clear views on the Middle East situation?

Jonathan, being young and handsome, laughed lightly in a debonair sort of way. 'I wouldn't say she was open-minded on the Middle East so much as empty-headed,' he smiled, possibly flicking a fleck of dust from his sleeve as he did so. 'For instance,' he added, carried away with his own wit, 'she probably thinks that Sinai is the plural of sinus.'

It's true that Riyadh's English-language newspaper is not essential reading in Westminster, and none of this might have caused Jonathan any loss of sleep had *Private Eye* – ever alert to a clanger or a cock-up – not chanced upon it and whooped with glee, Carol's mother by now having ascended to the leadership of the Conservative Party. Jonathan remained unperturbed, however, and continued in this vein until he was buttonholed by the Commons' chief whip, Airey Neave, who wasn't looking his most welcoming and hospitable and it seemed had not dropped by for a chat about shadow-cabinet prospects. With glacial calm, Neave enquired as to whether or not the reports in *Private Eye* were, by any outside chance, accurate. If they were, he confided, Mrs Thatcher would like an apology.

'Right-ho,' said Jonathan, or words to that effect. 'I'll drop her a line. I was just being lighthearted, don't you know?' And with that he prepared to saunter on his way.

A claw around his wrist prevented immediate escape. 'That will not do,' said the determined Mr Neave. 'She requires an apology in person.'

'Right-ho,' said Jonathan. 'I'll have a word next time I bump into her.' (This might not have been his precise response but, according to Simon Hoggart, it's a close approximation.)

The steel grip did not relax its hold. 'Nor will that do, I fear,' said the persistent Mr Neave. 'She has asked me to tell you that she will see you in the Lobby tonight after the 10.15 division. She will be wearing green.'

Jonathan thereupon became one of the first of many to be given a rehearsal of what the Day of Judgement could be like. No one was present to record his appearance as he staggered away from his handbagging by Mrs Thatcher that evening, but it's a safe bet that he was feeling rather like Bertie Wooster did after confronting Aunt Agatha.

Four years later, Mrs T became prime minister. By then, Jonathan was – perhaps wisely – married to someone other than Attila the Hen's daughter. In any case, he was no doubt grateful to have escaped having a mother-in-law who was a permanent reminder of his *faux pas* in Saudi Arabia. It has been said Mrs Thatcher had 'a memory that made an elephant seem scatter-brained', so it was hardly surprising that, after the Tories' victory in the 1979 general election, there was no ensuing ministerial appointment for Mr Aitken.

'Before The Truth Has Got Its Boots On'

The *Sun* Sells Jim Callaghan Down The River (1978)

Did he say it or didn't he? Did Prime Minister Jim Callaghan return from a world summit meeting in the West Indies at the height of the so-called 'winter of discontent' and, metaphorically putting the Nelsonian telescope to his eye, exclaim, 'Crisis? What crisis?' It depended, of course, on what one wanted to believe.

In 1976, when Harold Wilson resigned unexpectedly, 'Sunny' Jim Callaghan seemed the outsider in the contest to take over the helm of government as Britain's economic woes deepened. Once more there was a sterling crisis (see the section titled 'Wilson Devalues His Credibility', p. 49), but sterling crises had become as familiar a part of British life in the 1970s as fish and chips, and just as bad for your health. This time, however, Britain – a supposedly wealthy country – was in the humiliating position of needing the International Monetary Fund to bail it out. The nation had become, in fact, the acknowledged and derided 'sick man of Europe', suffering from constant strikes, low productivity and – not too many months earlier – an inability to keep the lights burning for more than three days of work a week (see the section titled 'Who's In Charge Around Here?', p. 67). But in Labour's leadership contest Callaghan won through because, aided by his no-nonsense, avuncular manner, he represented the best prospect of compromise in the struggle to keep the party's warring factions apart. The fact that he was, at six feet one inch, the tallest prime minister in British history was thought to be incidental.

The chalice handed to the new premier, if not exactly poisoned, was nevertheless pretty unpalatable. The price of IMF intervention was predictable: spending cuts, pay restraint and general belt-tightening. Equally predictable was the response of the trades unions, who in many people's opinion had become the true rulers of the land and were in no mood to accept restraints, which they felt were other people's problem. Indeed, by the end of 1978, union militancy had reached the point at which mounds of rotting garbage lay uncollected in the streets of some cities, hospitals were understaffed and corpses lay unburied as gravediggers downed their spades. The winter of discontent had settled on the nation.

In the meantime, Jim Callaghan set off for the Caribbean to take his place at a summit of world leaders in Guadeloupe. On his return, he was ambushed at Heathrow Airport by reporters who, naturally enough, were concerned about the mounting chaos at home and pressed him on the subject. Choosing his reply carefully, Sunny Jim said, 'I promise, if you look at it from the outside, I don't think other people in the world would share the view that there's mounting chaos.'

This was not, admittedly, a very illuminating or decisive answer; it was instead a politician's response – that is, it said nothing – and Callaghan was especially good at those. (He was, after all, the man whom Robin Day had once goaded in a broadcast interview with the same question seven consecutive times and yet still failed to provoke an answer.) This wasn't good enough for the *Sun*, however, who, like the tabloids of today, worked on the basis that, if a politician didn't say what you wanted him to say, you made it up. 'CRISIS? WHAT CRISIS?' screamed its headline the next day, provoking anger and disdain from those who were struggling to survive what looked like the disintegration of services in the middle of winter.

The irony was that only a month or two earlier, in September 1978, it had been widely expected that Callaghan would call a snap election, which the opinion polls suggested he might have won, but he had declined to take the risk. Now the best he could do was soldier on, trying to contain the damage of the winter of discontent.

It was a forlorn hope. Discontent of another kind now gripped even many union members, dismayed by the way in which their own leaders were holding the country to ransom and by the failure of the Labour government to curb them. In early 1979, Callaghan called for a vote of confidence in the Commons and lost it by a single vote. It was the first time in half a century a sitting government had lost such a vote.

Callaghan was forced to call a general election, which ushered in Margaret Thatcher and the Conservatives for the next eighteen years. The *Sun*'s headline, some would have said, played a big part in preparing the way. The last word, though, could go to Sunny Jim himself; 'A lie,' he once said, 'can be halfway around the world before the truth has got its boots on.'

The BBC Torpedoes The European Parliament

Reporting On The UK's MEPs In Strasbourg (1979)

It's never clear what the BBC will consider its most important duty to the nation. The rest of the world might have its eyes fixed firmly on sensational doings in, say, the United States or China, but once Auntie has decided that some other form of medicine is required she snaps her skirts around her thickening ankles in preparation for forcing lashings of it down the throats of Britain's viewers. And as the 1970s proceeded, she made it clear that Europe was the region her nieces and nephews had to learn to know and love, like it or not. France had at long last been forced to concede that Britain might, after all, have a tenuous connection to Europe and should therefore be allowed to join the Franco-German club known as the EEC (provided it behaved itself very well and never questioned the Common Agricultural Policy). In 1979, therefore, the BBC decreed that the activities of the European Parliament was a subject that the British public was longing to learn all about. It found an empty office in Broadcasting House to act as a studio, installed a correspondent and a producer or two, took out a subscription to *Le Monde* and prepared to enthral the nation.

So far, so good, despite the slight problem that the European parliament sat for only one week each month. A somewhat bigger headache was that the parliament catered for speakers of ten different languages, and fluency in any language other than English is not the hallmark of the British public. Of course, there were experienced translators hard at work in the parliament, but, as anyone who has had experience of translators coping with speeches and extempore contributions knows, simultaneous translation can often sound flat and boring. It was therefore decided that the BBC's studio should record both speaker and translator, enabling the producer to fade from one to the other as he saw fit. And so a member of staff was dispatched to Tottenham Court Road to buy a stereo tape recorder, which gave the BBC one track for the speaker and the other for the translator. It might not sound like much in today's climate of technical wizardry, but it seemed to be a good solution at the time.

The great day dawned when the BBC was to broadcast the European Parliament for the first time. On that occasion, there was an unusually well-attended and, to all appearances, lively debate in progress. With a mixture of excitement and apprehension, the new equipment was plugged in – but, to their surprise, the BBC crew could hear nothing. Worse still, things seemed to be going wrong on the floor of the parliament. The debate seemed to have stopped in full flight. MEPs began to take off their headphones and frown at them or tap them, shaking first them and then their heads, and then complaining to the parliament's president. It seemed as though the session was about to be suspended.

'Then came the awful realisation,' wrote BBC correspondent John Sergeant, 'that our equipment, bought with such pride in Tottenham Court Road, had torpedoed the workings of the European Community.'

Indeed, the moment the tape recorder had been plugged in, all ten translations were channelled into the members' headphones at once. The MEPs were, in a very real sense, getting simultaneous pan-European translations on a grand scale. The BBC quickly pulled the plug and calm and order was instantly restored.

And so it was that, on its very first attempt at tapping into the EC, the UK introduced the buggeration factor into all matters European – an act that, it could be said, it has subsequently turned into a tradition.

'Grotesque, Unbelievable, Bizarre And Unprecedented'

Naughty Charlie Haughey And His Irish Shenanigans (1979–92)

'Ireland is where strange tales begin and happy endings are possible,' Charles Haughey once said. Well, in his own case he got the first part right, but the happy endings didn't quite work out as planned. Adept at forging political alliances and fixing people and things behind the scenes, Charlie (as he was affectionately known in the years before his misdemeanours started to come to light) got to the top of the greasy pole four times between 1979 and 1992. In other words, he was the republic of Ireland's 'taoiseach', which, when pronounced correctly as *tee-shock*, might sound like the moment you hook your drive into a lake but is actually Gaelic for 'prime minister'.

As it turned out, Charlie – or 'Sweetie', as it later transpired he was called in certain situations – had interests in areas other than political power alone. Wealth, too, was a subject just as close to his heart, and he accumulated a Georgian mansion in Dublin, a large stud farm and, for good measure, the entire island of Innisvickalaun, just off the Kerry coast.

The earlier scandals in which Charlie got embroiled, though, were concerned less with profit than with politics. As Northern Ireland erupted in violence towards the end of the 1960s, he advocated military invasion and, putting other peoples' money where his mouth was, became involved (or so it was widely said at the time) in employing an aid fund intended for civil use to purchase guns for IRA hit men. The ensuing uproar left him in the political wilderness for a decade.

To an outsider, Irish politics of the 1970s seemed like an elaborate game of musical chairs in which, on every third Wednesday of a month containing the letter M (or, failing that, J), the two main parties – Fianna Fáil and Fine Gael – changed places with the assistance of a minor party, thus acquiring a majority of one or, in a really good year, two. Whoever held power at any given moment, therefore, was likely to have a short life span, and trying to prolong this was a continuous preoccupation.

Charlie thought it would be a wizard idea to keep track of what political journalists were up to by tapping their phones, and proceeded to implement such a plan with some *brio*. When this, too, came to light, there was further uproar (a condition that assails Irish politicians at regular intervals) and Charlie found himself having to practise his sincere and honest look as he appeared before the cameras, insisting it must have been the other fellow. The unfortunate 'other fellow' in this case was named as Minister for Justice Sean Doherty, who duly walked the plank in 1982 but had his revenge ten years later, in 1992, when Haughey's hold on power was hanging by a thread. At that time, Doherty admitted that he'd covered up for Charlie, who had actually authorised the whole thing. The thread snapped and Haughey fell.

The question was, had Haughey fallen for the last time or could this Irish Houdini regain power for a fifth? As one of Ireland's most distinguished sons, Conor Cruise O'Brien, once said, 'If I saw Mr Haughey buried at midnight at a crossroads with a stake driven through his heart – politically speaking – I should continue to wear garlic around my neck, just in case.'

It was at this time that the rumours of Charlie's dodgy dealings took substance, allowing O'Brien to dispense with his clove of garlic. It wasn't that whispers of scandal had been absent during his years of leadership; indeed, like worms taking a periodic peek above ground to see if it was still raining, they had surfaced with some regularity. When questioned on one occasion about certain 'irregularities' in the period 1982–7, Charlie scotched such rumours as being 'grotesque, unbelievable, bizarre and unprecedented' – well-chosen words, as it later turned out, but not in the way he intended them to be taken.

Matters began to unravel when Ben Dunne, owner of a chain of supermarkets, became embroiled in a battle to retain control of his business. He revealed in court that he'd handed over as much as £1.3 million to Charlie to keep him suitably open-minded and pliable. Charlie's adoring Irish public – or, at least, that section of it that had believed in him – was somewhat less than pleased as, during his first two terms as taoiseach, he had devoted a significant proportion of his time to instructing people to pull their belts several notches tighter. 'As a community, we are living away beyond our means . . . at a rate which is simply not justifiable,' he had thundered in a speech to the nation in 1980. Yet now it was revealed that Charlie had found ways around the problem not open to the populace at large. Had the rumours about his addiction to schemes for self-improvement been right all along?

It was decided that the question of corruption in Irish politics should be thoroughly investigated, and the McCracken and Moriarty Tribunals were set up to do so. Soon after they began their investigations, all sorts of naughtiness began to emerge. First of all, it seemed that Charlie had devoted considerable sums of Fianna Fáil party funds to the purchase of Charvet shirts from Paris. (One must, after all, be well-dressed when using further sums of money from the same source to entertain in the very best Dublin restaurants.) Then there was the matter of a wee loan of £1 million from the Allied Irish Bank, of which he had been let off £400,000 on being appointed taoiseach for the first time in 1979. Why? What services had been rendered for such forgiving behaviour from, of all institutions, a bank?

It was clear that Haughey had been a very proper Charlie indeed, and at one point he was besieged by an angry crowd at Dublin Castle. Despite Haughey's attempts to frustrate it (for which he was threatened with criminal charges), the Moriarty Tribunal revealed that £8 million had been paid to him over an eighteen-year period by businessmen seeking – and getting – political favours.

In 1999, the icing on the revelation cake was added when a gossip columnist named Terry Keane appeared on Irish TVs *Late, Late Show* and told the waiting world that the 'Sweetie' to whom she had often referred in her column was none other than Charlie Haughey, with whom – unbeknown to his wife and family – she had been conducting an affair for more than quarter of a century. The once-admired leader had now become an object of open ridicule.

The Mad Monk Comes To The Aid Of British Industry

Sir Keith Joseph Airs His Views On The New Mini Metro (1980)

Sir Keith Joseph was the *éminence grise* behind Mrs Thatcher's first Tory administration following her success in the UK's 1979 general election. He read copiously, thought a lot (sometimes even about relevant matters), did his own shopping, ate little and looked gaunt and woebegone much of the time. On one occasion, when a group of political correspondents was using him as an excuse for a slap-up meal at one of London's most expensive restaurants, he baffled them all by ordering a slice of British Rail cake for his dinner. A piece of fruit-and-nut was duly delivered, the waiter having thoughtfully removed the plastic wrapping first (if he hadn't, his customer might not even have noticed). Sir Keith picked his way slowly through it while the assorted journalists tucked into the oysters and tournedos they'd had in their sights from the outset.

Being an *éminence grise* puts heavy demands on the nervous system, and Sir Keith could from time to time be seen gently beating his head against the wall. Equally, he might rise from his desk or the cabinet table without warning in the middle of a meeting and walk up and down the room, smiting his forehead in an attempt to force yet more eminent thoughts from his little grey cells. Not surprisingly, he was quickly christened 'the Mad Monk' by his irreverent colleagues and by even less reverent journalists.

Throughout his bouts of eccentric behaviour, however, Sir Keith could be relied upon to retain absolute honesty, and he invariably displayed a candour that was positively unnerving to the rest of the political world, accustomed as it was to providing devious answers to questions as straightforward as 'How are you today?' This was all very well – even praiseworthy, in a way – but if you're secretary of state for industry, complete honesty can, on occasion, be a trifle misplaced.

It had been well-known for more than a generation that the British car industry was a hopeless cause if foreign manufacturers didn't step in to demonstrate how it should be done. No political party ever had the courage to tell it as it was, however, and so they were all obliged to subscribe to the myth that the next new model would show the world just how good the UK really was at making a car that remained roadworthy for more than five days at a time.

Not all that long after he'd taken office, Sir Keith's engagement secretary informed him that British Leyland's new Mini Metro was to be launched that day and he was scheduled for an interview with Granada TV to extol its charm and brilliance to the skies. Before the Mad Monk had time to open his mouth in protest, she had wheeled on her elegant heel and left the room.

'Was the Mini Metro not a wonderful new car? And wasn't it going to be the salvation of the British car industry,' the interviewer demanded to know of the Secretary of State for Industry, anticipating a five-minute monologue on the new dawn of this vital enterprise on which so many Midlands jobs depended.

'Um, I don't know,' said Sir Keith with disarming frankness.

Roused unanticipated into action, the interviewer tried again: 'Surely, the new Mini Metro was setting new standards in car design and production? Was it not bound to be the envy of the worldwide car-manufacturing industry?'

Sir Keith fidgeted unhappily. 'You're asking the wrong man,' he answered with the air of someone hoping to be somewhere else very shortly.

The interviewer began to perspire gently. 'But surely—' he began, just as the Secretary of State for Industry decided that utter candour was what was needed in this situation: 'You see, I don't know anything about cars. I haven't even owned one for five years, since mine was stolen.'

The interviewer made one last, manic attempt to salvage the interview he had confidently expected to be a breeze. 'But you must have ridden in a car,' he said, his voice ascending the octave despairingly. 'You know, tried out the controls, that kind of thing?'

Sir Keith pondered deeply. 'Er, well, no. I haven't, really. I haven't seen . . . I don't know . . . Oh dear. You'll have to stop.'

And that was that. Sir Keith had done everything we demand of politicians – he had told the truth, the whole truth and nothing but the truth – and yet it left people feeling thoroughly dissatisfied. If only we demanded of our politicians that they tell us lies, damned lies and nothing but damned lies, we'd hardly ever be disappointed.

Cecil Loses The Keays Of Office

Cecil Parkinson Resigns (October 1983)

Distinguished *Times* feature- and editorial-writer Bernard Levin once said of Cecil Parkinson that there were three strong women in his life – Margaret Thatcher, his political boss; Ann, his wife; and Sarah Keays, his secretary – and whatever he did appeared to be the result of whichever of them had spoken severely to him most recently. If there was any truth in this, it appeared to serve Cecil just fine until, in 1983, he found himself piggy in the middle of this formidable triangle.

Cecil had risen to fame in the Conservative Party and, more critically, in Margaret Thatcher's eyes by running the Tories' successful general-election campaign in 1979. His reward was a place in the Cabinet and in the affections of his leader, a woman who trusted only a few of those around her. To be sure, he did himself no harm thereafter by agreeing with everything she said, which was no less than was expected of him; and not once, either in public or in private, was he discovered being 'wet', a term of abuse so powerful among the Tories of the 1980s that children were sent to bed early to avoid the risk of overhearing it after the watershed. So, as October 1983 dawned, he was secretary of state for trade and industry and the darling of true-blue conference-goers the length and breadth of the UK.

It was on 5 October that a cloud no bigger than a man's (let's be careful here) hand appeared on the horizon. A rumour began to circulate that Cecil was having an affair with his secretary, Sarah Keays. In response, Mr

Parkinson furrowed his brow in his well-practised concerned yet sincere look, which implied, 'Would I do such a thing?'

The gossip continued to whisper along the corridors of Westminster, however, and lobby correspondents began to ask themselves whether or not that well-rehearsed excuse for publishing rumour – 'the public interest' – was now upon them.

Mr P felt obliged to issue a statement in which he admitted to the affair. The true-blue party workers were not a whit dismayed, as far as anyone could discern. A fond smile, a shake of the head and a general murmur of 'Well, boys will be boys, won't they?' appeared to be the reaction.

Meanwhile, Miss Keays smouldered quietly in private but kept her ammunition dry until the critical moment. When she finally chose to light the blue touchpaper, she enjoyed rather more success than Guy Fawkes had achieved 378 years earlier. She waited until the Tory faithful were assembled for the annual party conference before calling the gentlemen of the press to her side. She had perceived she said that the full facts had not been made public, and that Mr P had not been as frank about the affair as he had claimed. Media comment, continued speculation and government pronouncements (meaning, presumably, 'family values', 'sanctity of marriage' and so forth) had placed her in 'an impossible position'.

But have you any real proof of this? the gentlemen of the press enquired, no doubt in the solicitous and caring way for which they are renowned the world over.

Well, yes, Sarah replied. She was carrying Cecil's child. 'My baby was conceived in a longstanding, loving relationship,' she explained, 'which I allowed to continue because I believed in our eventual marriage.' Before a single reporter could exclaim, 'There's one born every minute,' she went on to explain that Cecil had proposed to her not once but twice during their twelve-year affair but had changed his mind on both occasions.

Now this was a story. Even Mr P recognised that he couldn't wriggle out of this one and sought out his beloved leader in her hotel room, resignation letter in hand, to explain how naughty he'd been. Mrs T accepted that he'd have to go, at least for a while, although her general attitude seemed to be a somewhat sorrowful 'Well, boys will be boys, I suppose.'

Friends of Mr P allowed it to be known that he was 'quite broken' by what had happened, though if that was true then it seemed most likely to have been the result of his subsequent encounter with his wife, Ann. To be sure, she wasn't seen in public brandishing a rolling pin, but anything was possible behind the scenes. It was reported in the press that 'reporters assembled outside [Cecil and Ann's] Hertfordshire home', whereas in fact they did rather more than assemble, they swarmed over the garden and put ladders against the walls, hoping to record the sound of heavy objects striking bone, but without success.

Sarah Keays' baby was born on New Year's Eve, 1983. Mrs P ordered Mr P to remain married to her, so he did. Mrs Thatcher gave him a four-year sabbatical, so off he went, eventually rejoining the Cabinet in 1987. Boys will, after all, be boys. Then, in 1997, he became chairman of the Conservative Party and was told to accept a life peerage, so he did. One wonders what Sarah Keays and her child, now in her twenties, think of it all.

Caught In A Wright Old Mess

The British Government Attempts To Ban 'Spycatcher' (1987)

Peter Wright joined GCHQ (Government Communication Headquarters) after World War II and, in due course, transferred to be a 'secret-service operative' in MI5, the undercover organisation devoted to maintaining Britain's internal security. A fair chunk of his career was spent hunting Russian moles in the organisation, a matter about which the press exercised an obsessive interest following the high-profile defection of Burgess, MacLean and Philby to the Soviets. Even spies, it turned out, have to hang up their bowlers and umbrellas when they reach the age of 65 and are expected to retire discreetly into the sunset, pretending that they've devoted their lives to banking or the insurance industry.

When Peter Wright queued up for his gold watch in 1982, however, he found that his pension package wasn't all that he'd anticipated. The government of the day decreed that the pension he'd earned from his early days at GCHQ wasn't transferable, thus diminishing the comfort he had anticipated in old age. He withdrew to Tasmania, smarting, and planned a revenge that would, with luck, earn him a windfall in compensation. And so it was that he wrote *Spycatcher*, a book about his time at MI5.

The book wasn't particularly good, being full of unsubstantiated madcap plans to bug conferences and assassinate President Nasser of Egypt, not to mention an unlikely plot to paint former Labour prime minister Harold Wilson as a Russian spy and, best of all, to prove that the head of MI5 itself was a Soviet mole. It did, though, contain more reliable information about MI5's techniques and practices.

Unsurprisingly, the British government was less than keen that the book be read by its citizens and in 1985 banned its publication in the UK. This wasn't a particularly good move given that (a) most countries in the world have a publishing industry; (b) many of the inhabitants of those countries can read English, and a translation can easily be provided for those who don't; and (c) there's nothing like a good old ban to provide instant publicity and ensure that the book will sell three times the number it would have done otherwise. If the government had said something like, 'Well, Peter Wright seems to have made most of it up, as you can see, but, if you enjoy fairy tales, go ahead,' *Spycatcher* would probably have joined the pile of remaindered books being flogged off cheap within twelve months. As it was, editions of it began to spring up everywhere like mushrooms – except, of course, in Britain.

In late 1985, the British attorney general Sir Patrick Mayhew lodged a case against Wright in Australia, where he then lived, in an attempt to prevent publication in that country, and over the course of the next eighteen months he also launched seven actions against British newspapers – including the *Sunday Times,* the *Telegraph,* the *Observer* and the *Guardian* – in order to prevent them from publishing extracts from the book. Roy Hattersley accused the Tory government of 'behaving in a scandalous way when it must have known it would lose in the end'. Even as he spoke, an American edition – initially of 100,000 copies – was being readied for publication stateside while Ireland and the Netherlands were well ahead in the race to profit from the helpful publicity being so readily provided by the UK's attorney general. Travellers to Ireland and North America were returning with copies of the book to sell on to their friends and relations at home, and by the time the British case against Peter Wright and the Australian publisher came to court, half the world and a sizeable chunk of the British public had read it.

The hearing in Australia in September 1987 was notable for the pyrotechnic performance of Wright's advocate, a former journalist called

Malcolm Turnbull who, back in 1980, had decided to have a bash at a career in law. (After the case, having established his reputation, he promptly embarked on a third career, as a businessman, before adding a fourth in politics.) In the course of the hearing, Turnbull wrung from British civil servant Robert Armstrong the memorable admission that his government might have been 'economical with the truth', a phrase that passed instantly into the language and helped to ensure that the British case was lost.

Back in the UK in July, the *Sunday Times* had elected to proceed with serialisation of the US edition of *Spycatcher* (sales of which were by now approaching 400,000), whatever the outcome in the Australian courts. A British judge described the government's attempted injunction to prevent them from doing so as something that made the law 'an ass' when the American edition of the book was so easily available. Injunctions against other newspapers were quietly dropped and, by the autumn of 1987, the battle was effectively over. It was later estimated that the various legal attempts to prevent the publication of the book in Britain and Australia had cost the taxpayer around £1 million.

Moving with their customary stately measure (which nevertheless seems like the speed of light compared to the proceedings of the European Court of Human Rights), the law lords eventually got around to ruling on the matter in October 1988. Despite denouncing Peter Wright as a traitor over a year earlier, it was now decided that the public interest outweighed any threat to national security, a judgement that underlined the prescience of Roy Hattersley's much earlier words. It took the European Court a further three years to conclude that freedom of speech had been under threat.

Peter Wright, meanwhile, had achieved at least one of his objectives: he was now a millionaire, and must have wondered why he hadn't devoted his career to writing novels.

Edwina Lays An Egg

The Great Salmonella Scare (1988)

Salmonella is bacteria that causes a nasty form of food poisoning and, in a worst-case situation, can kill. Nor does it come in one neatly packaged form but, like all bugs, learns to diversify in different directions. During the Thatcher government, the sort that Parliamentary Undersecretary for Health Edwina Currie was talking about went under the alarming title of *Salmonella enteritidis* PT4 (i.e. phage type 4). If you didn't feel a little nauseous after trying to get your tongue around that mouthful, the effects of encountering it in a raw or undercooked egg were likely to make you a good deal sicker.

In the summer of 1988, that was exactly what Edwina and the DHSS (Department of Health and Social Security) were worried about. Whereas in 1982 there had been 413 cases of PT4, the first ten months of 1988 produced 10,544. This was bad enough, but what made it even more alarming was that this figure showed an increase of one hundred per cent on the position twelve months earlier. PT4, it seemed, had found a way of living in the laying hen and thus being present in the egg itself. In July and August of 1988, therefore, the British government issued public health warnings about the use of raw eggs.

As summer turned to autumn, it became apparent that it wasn't just raw eggs that contained the problem. An egg, it seemed, had to be cooked at a temperature of 80 degrees centigrade for at least a minute if the potential bug was to be killed off, so at the end of November a further warning – the fifth of the year – was issued, this time concerning lightly cooked as well

91

as raw eggs. The government, in the shape of MAFF (Ministry for Agriculture, Fisheries and Food), was doing its best to get the egg-producing industry to sit up and take notice of the problem, but its efforts appeared to be generating little response. However, one industry that was only too ready to leap into action was the media, which had since got wind of the problem (not that it needed to be especially alert, in view of the stream of warnings that were being issued) and was beginning to prowl the corridors of the Westminster chicken coop.

Edwina Currie knew that she would have to make a very public statement sooner or later; only for so long could she fend off the phone calls and enquiries by referring to the previous health warnings the government had issued. In any case, the egg farmers themselves seemed in no mood to take measures to overhaul their industry, and it looked as if they would have to be goaded into doing so under the weight of public insistence.

Edwina chose therefore a television interview with ITN on 3 December to raise the profile of the problem. She had no intention of being alarmist, and her aim was to put people on their guard and understand that eggs or, indeed, any product using eggs, should be cooked for at least one minute before consumption.

The interview appeared to go well but for one word that, in retrospect, caused great furore. In one reply to a question, Edwina said, 'We do warn people now that *most* of the egg production in this country, sadly, is now infested with salmonella.' This was reasonable enough, given that only the previous day the Welsh Public Health Laboratory had written that 'all eggs . . . should be regarded as possibly infected', although Edwina herself admitted later that it would have been safer had she said 'much' rather than 'most'. Unfortunately, by then the damage (to her) was done.

The implication that virtually the whole egg-producing industry was endangered turned the air blue with imprecations and curses. Suddenly it seemed that half the population (of people, that is, not hens) was in the egg-producing business, pausing from its labours only to stick pins in effigies of Edwina. Irate spokesmen (mainly) and spokeswomen (occasionally) grabbed the nearest microphone or sought the nearest camera to denounce the Undersecretary for bringing the industry to its knees (conveniently forgetting that egg consumption had been in steady decline for some years beforehand). Worse, many of these spokesfolk flatly denied that there was any infection of any kind – 'Not in my eggs, mate. Trust me!'

So how was it that there were all these salmonella PT4 cases? Glad you asked that. It all arises from faulty cooking, you see. Housewives with grubby hands; that kind of thing. What, when they're boiling an egg? Oh, yes. You really can't be too careful you know.

It wasn't long before the tabloids, in their usual scattergun approach, began to put words into Edwina's mouth that she hadn't actually said. 'Most eggs' were infected, for example, and 'don't buy eggs'. The government decided to keep calm, say nothing and let the storm blow over. But it didn't and, ten days after the by-now-notorious interview on ITN, Edwina Currie resigned.

No Miracles For The Blessed Margaret

Mrs Thatcher's Judgement Proves Fallible
(November 1990)

Two is, in most contexts, a small number. Not, perhaps, if you win the World Cup 2–1 or find you're expecting twins, but in terms of majorities in ballots or elections it's so insignificant as to be unworthy of notice. Or so the Blessed Margaret, as Mrs Thatcher was known to some of her party (in their more polite moments), would have said. Yet on a cold and ominous night outside the British Embassy in Paris in November 1990, it proved to be a fatal number.

By this time, Mrs T had been in office for eleven and a half years, for all but the last few months of which she had merrily handbagged anybody who stood in her way, be they Argentine generals, Arthur Scargill and the miners, wets in her own party, anybody in an opposition party or, indeed, anyone who failed to agree with her. For a while, though, and for the first time in her leadership of the Tory Party, she had begun to look vulnerable. The ill-advisedness of the 'Poll Tax', as the new Community Charge taxation scheme was quickly dubbed, had shaken her façade of apparent invulnerability. Sensing this, Michael Heseltine, erstwhile colleague turned implacable foe, was dogging her footsteps, awaiting his chance to drop out of a tree or leap from a bush and challenge her – or, better still, get someone else to do the heinous deed. The rumour-mills began to grind, foretelling the possibility of a challenge to Mrs T, and sure enough a challenge was mounted. A vote on her leadership was scheduled.

Meantime the diary-keeper informed her she was due in Paris to join the group of world leaders celebrating the fall of the Berlin Wall, the collapse of the Soviet Union and the end of the Cold War. Her best mates would be there – notably George Bush Sr and Mikhail Gorbachev – with some of her less beloved chums, including stroppy Europeans François Mitterand and Helmut Kohl. Clearly this was no time to stay cowering at home, looking scared of a few of one's own MPs. There were photo calls to attend and credit to be grabbed on behalf of Britain for a notable part in the endgame that promised to reunite Europe.

And so Mrs T took the fateful decision. She decreed the ballot should be run while she was in Paris being a world statesman. Even if there had been a smidgen of doubt that all but a handful of her loyal MPs would fall dutifully into line behind her leadership, they could not bring themselves to do so when their all-powerful Leaderine was being projected on the world's TV screens at her regal – nay, imperial – best and most commanding. Could they?

She had forgotten the old adage that when the cat's away the mice will play. Squeaking and chattering excitedly, a swarm of Tories emerged from the wainscoting and made for the ballot boxes. The result was announced even as Mrs T was putting a fresh set of weights into her handbag in the British Embassy, prior to setting out for a banquet with her world-famous chums in the splendour of Versailles. In cold figures, the outcome was: Margaret Thatcher, 204; Michael Heseltine, 152; abstentions, 16.

Although on the face of it Mrs T had won the ballot by 54 votes, there were a few buts. In the first place, it was an unspoken truism that, if more than a hundred of his or her own party voted against the leader of the day, he or she was seriously weakened. Secondly, there was a rule in force that, in order to win outright, without the need for a second ballot, the victor must have not only a clear majority but an additional fifteen per cent of those entitled to vote. On this calculation, Mrs Thatcher needed to win by 56 votes to avoid a second ballot, so she was short by two, a number that would seem scarcely worth noticing in most contexts but was fatal in this one.

Mrs Thatcher put a grim but brave face on it in the cold night air of Paris. She announced to a flabbergasted world that she would, of course, go forward with confidence to the second ballot. Even so, it's unlikely that she much enjoyed her banquet at Versailles that evening. As she picked the bones from her fish, she must have reflected that, had her hubris not decreed that the ballot be held while she was away from Westminster, she would have had little difficulty in quelling the rebellion with a few direct and well-chosen words.

As it was, soundings taken when she returned to London quickly showed that the chattering mice of yesterday now looked more like sharks gathering at the smell of blood in the water. Her previously faithful followers recognised the scent of a fatally wounded prey. It was the end. On November 22nd the anniversary of President Kennedy's rather more terminal assassination 27 years earlier, Mrs Thatcher departed to start work on her memoirs.

She's Behind You!

John Sergeant Fails To Notice A World Exclusive Bearing Down On Him (1990)

While Mrs T was inadvertently moving towards her Waterloo in Paris, the BBC was debating whether or not it was worth deploying their Chief Political Correspondent, John Sergeant, to cover the anticipated orgy of backslapping among the world leaders. After all, back home in the Westminster village, events of a more titillating nature – i.e. the notorious ballot on the Tory Party leadership (see previous chapter) – were developing. Mrs T surely wasn't going to lose; the only newsworthy issue would be the size of the rebellion, out of which more mileage might be wrung than from a glamorous but ultimately uneventful jamboree in Paris. Finger-ends were sucked at the BBC and it was eventually decided to hold the Political Editor, John Cole, in London and to despatch Sergeant to Paris. To ensure that there was no unseemly excess of expenditure, he would be working with a French cameraman, and it would be fair to say that the amount of communication between them was less than minimal.

In Paris the day passed uneventfully, but in Westminster tension was growing fast as whispers began to arise towards evening that the ballot was looking interesting. John Sergeant proceeded to the British Embassy, from whence Mrs T was expected to issue on her way to a state banquet. As Westminster whispers turned to solid words however, and reached the ears of those gathered around the embassy, the traditional battle for supremacy between the TV and press reporters was this time won by the former. The police herded the journalists behind crush barriers out on the wings and left the media interviewers and camera crews inside.

Soon, news of the result and the likelihood of a second ballot was out in the open. Back home the BBC's *Six O'Clock News* was rolling and the studio decided to extend it beyond the normal 6:30 close in case there was a chance that Mrs Thatcher might be persuaded to comment.

John Sergeant duly positioned himself with his back to the Embassy steps and facing his French cameraman to give his report. He had been advised by an official from the Foreign Office that it would be a good half hour before Mrs Thatcher came out. This seemed realistic, for she would surely be on the phone to Downing Street getting an assessment of the situation.

At that moment, however, John got word through his earpiece that he was on live and began to talk. Mrs Thatcher would not be coming out in the foreseeable future, he informed the watching hordes, explaining her need to consult, think out her position, etc., etc.

Meanwhile, the 13 million viewers back home saw the prime minister advancing down the steps of the embassy behind Sergeant's back, accompanied by her press secretary, Bernard Ingham. As she loomed more and more into camera shot, Sergeant warmed to his theme. At that very moment, he explained, the PM would be assessing the import of this surprising ballot outcome.

Meanwhile, Peter Sissons in the studio was yelling, 'She's behind you, John!' into his earpiece, but the link had gone and Sergeant heard nothing. Photographers began jumping up and down and gesticulating. What on earth is happening? Sergeant thought to himself.

The first rule of speaking to camera with an appearance of gravitas is never to look behind you, but some sixth sense prompted him to break it. He turned and, to his horror, saw Mrs T in full sail right behind him. It was, as he said later, 'pure pantomime'.

'Where's the microphone?' growled Ingham, pushing Sergeant roughly to one side. It occurred to the latter that this was a damn fool question, since he was holding it.

'Prime Minister, it's here. This is the microphone,' he said, pushing it under her nose, whereupon she delivered her famous pronouncement that she was pleased to have got more than half the votes and would be going forward to the second ballot. With that, she and Ingham turned smartly about and marched back into the embassy, leaving the BBC with its best scoop in years.

It was the very hurriedness of the whole scene that finally undermined Mrs Thatcher. Her intention had been to go over to the phalanx of press reporters and make a single statement to them all, but when the footage of the event was played back it was immediately obvious that viewers had seen something quite different. They had seen a Prime Minister who did not know where the microphone she sought actually was, accompanied by an aide who roughly manhandled people in his way. The appearance was that of a politician who had lost her grip. As John Sergeant wrote in his autobiography, 'Like a political cartoon, a devastatingly accurate caricature had been created.'

As for the reputation of the Chief Political Correspondent who seconds earlier appeared to have egg all over his face as he informed the world that nothing was happening when the opposite was visibly true, a rival from another channel summed it all up: 'You're going to be famous for making a bloody mistake.' Sergeant did indeed become famous, but thanks to Mrs T the mistake was forgotten.

'I've Got A Little List'

Peter Lilley Has A Moment He'd Rather Forget
(1992)

No political party should be in office for more than two terms, preferably short ones. The effect of having their snouts submerged in the trough of perks and power makes ministers forget what life is really like beyond the inner suburbs of London.

This was certainly true of the Conservatives after Neil Kinnock and Old Labour contrived – against all expectations – to hand them a fourth straight election victory in April 1992. Their party conference the following October saw them at their detached and triumphant worst, as Peter Lilley proceeded to demonstrate.

In part, at least, Lilley owed the fact that he was on the platform at all to Nicholas Ridley, the prototypical grumpy old man. Two years earlier, as Secretary of State for Trade and Industry, he had relieved himself in public of some profound thoughts about Britain's German partners in the European Union. Their proposal for Economic and Monetary Union was, he growled, 'a German racket designed to take over the whole of Europe'. Since this was, in all probability, true, nobody objected to that bit, but he spoiled it by going on to say that giving up sovereignty to Europe was as bad as giving it up to Adolf Hitler. The resulting storm did more than ruffle feathers; it denuded chickens in barnyards across the Continent. It also blew Ridley out of office, to be replaced by the youthful-looking Peter Lilley. The boy done well at the DTI, or so it was considered, so after the election he was moved to the Department of Social Security and given licence to declare war on scroungers, spongers, the unemployed and ne'er-do-wells in general.

This is a familiar war that has been fought across the political generations, as eagerly today as ever, but Peter Lilley chose a crass way to go about presenting his credentials as the umpteenth tough general who would wade into battle against the foe. Given that the average age of the audience at these annual party shindigs is touching eighty, part of the challenge for any speaker – especially in the graveyard session after lunch – is keeping them awake long enough to remember who you are.

The new secretary of state decided that the ditty from Gilbert and Sullivan's *Mikado* that begins 'I've got a little list of those who won't be missed' was just the thing to appeal to a certain generation, so he composed some new words and opened his mouth. It would have been an ill-advised tactic even had he had a voice to rival a seraph – or, at worst, a cherub – but in practice he was more of a corncrake than the ageing Mick Jagger. It was a bad start, made worse by the words.

Let us not, at any price, do justice to the foolishness of it all by repeating the whole ghastly thing. A single example, to give the flavour, is more than enough: 'I've got a little list,' went one refrain, 'of young ladies who get pregnant just to jump the housing list.' It goes without saying that the assembled delegates loved it and the rest of the country was repelled by it.

If you gave Peter Lilley his time again, he would certainly wish he'd been persuaded not to open his mouth that day. Indeed, once he left ministerial office behind, he became the very model of a thoughtful MP. As Labour member Paul Flynn put it, once 'his ministerial lobotomy was reversed, Peter has spoken with courage and conviction' on a number of important issues, notably the legalisation of cannabis in 2001 and in the considered and independently minded report he produced in 2005 on the issue of identity cards.

If Ned Sherrin is to be believed, however, (and why not?) Lilley did receive a comeuppance of a sort not so very long after that infamous party conference. A couple of years later he was at a reception and among the guests was the author Peter Ackroyd, who is openly gay. Spotting the still youthful-looking (despite his 51 years) Peter Lilley across the room, he marched over to make his acquaintance. 'And what do you do?' he enquired as an opening gambit.

'Social Security,' Lilley replied truthfully, for he was – despite the Gilbert and Sullivan – still in office.

'You poor boy,' Ackroyd rejoined. 'Come home with me and we'll see what we can do about it.'

'Thick-skinned, Short-sighted And Always Ready To Charge'

David Mellor Resigns (September 1992)

David Mellor was one of those politicians who provoked wholehearted responses: you either loved or hated his gap-toothed grin and provocative manner as he hurled himself wholeheartedly into the latest controversy. Trained as yet another person designed to be a burden on the nation's GDP, that is to say a lawyer, he once described members of his profession as 'like rhinoceroses: thick-skinned, short-sighted and always ready to charge'. It could be the pithiest autobiography in history, the perfect description of the image he himself projected. He could be, and frequently was, insensitive and impatient, arrogant and brutal, and yet – intellectually and in his political causes – often liberal and humane, quick-witted and entertaining.

Mellor entered parliament in 1979, and by 1990 he was in the Cabinet as chief secretary to the Treasury. That same year he was one of the architects of the controversial deregulatory Broadcasting Act that opened ITV contracts to competitive bidding and changed Channel 4 into a public corporation. Straight away, therefore, he contrived to make as many enemies as friends among media folk and Islington's celebrated 'chattering classes'.

This, it transpired, was merely a foretaste of what was to come two years later. By 1992 he had progressed to being Secretary of State for National Heritage, a job created especially for him that covered broadcasting, heritage, the arts and the media in general. He was instantly dubbed the 'minister for fun', and indeed he had hardly settled behind his desk when the fun began in earnest.

Under pressure from his parliamentary colleagues to crack down on press intrusion into private life – something, it was felt, that was getting out of hand – he launched an assault on the gentlemen of the fourth estate. Many ordinary punters would have agreed with the premise but, at a time when the Labour opposition was beginning to throw accusations of sleaze across the debating chamber, it was dangerous to suggest that the press should be reined in by legislation. Mellor himself had never been a proponent of such an approach – no doubt seeing the dangers of state interference through a lawyer's eyes – but, in an attempt to forewarn the press of the parliamentary pressures building up, he issued his celebrated warning to them, and to the tabloids in particular, that they were 'drinking in the last chance saloon'. Any more excessive intrusions into people's private lives, the message went, and legislation might become unstoppable.

Now, if there's one thing editors and journalists cannot abide at any price, it is being criticised. In their world, they are righteous and the rest of the world is perennially sacrilegious, so the 'last chance saloon' remark was worse than a red rag to a bull. They sharpened their pencils and made ready for war.

They need not have bothered. The minister for fun was, at that very moment, having a rollicking time of his own in the saloon. Scarcely had he ordered drinks all round and raised his glass with a toast to Antonia de Sancha – a hitherto unknown actress – than news of his affair with her was all over the *People*, that notorious rock of British morality. The newspaper had been tipped off – by Miss de Sancha's landlord, as it transpired, rather than by the lady herself – and in its zeal to stand upon the moral high ground (sometimes referred to as 'selling more copies') had paid said landlord to let them bug her flat without her knowledge. When the paper ran the story in July 1992, she was as devastated as Mr Mellor, but, as the *People*'s editor, Bill Hagerty, kindly explained in case readers naïvely supposed that he was interested only in sales, he felt that the matter was 'in the public interest'. David Mellor promptly offered his resignation to the Prime Minister, but, since the affair was entirely unconnected with Mellor's job, John Major refused it. To the press, that was like the prick of a picador's spear.

They wanted Mellor out of the way because he had dared threaten their own power, and for the next two months – right through the August silly season and into the autumn – the story ran and ran, scaling ever higher peaks of absurdity as it did so. Mr Mellor posed with his wife and children for one paper while his father-in-law denounced him to another.

Meanwhile, Miss de Sancha, thrown to the wolves by her landlord's betrayal and her lover's abandonment, turned for help to any quarter that offered it. Regrettably for her and the truth, she found it in the offices of Max Clifford, a soi-disant publicist who derives a substantial part of his livelihood from tossing morsels to the piranhas otherwise known as the tabloids. By the time Miss de Sancha was hauled from the water, her character had been stripped to the bone.

As the summer wore on, the claims appearing in the papers below Miss de Sancha's name oscillated between the hilarious and the ludicrous. Mr Mellor had insisted on making love to her not merely in a Chelsea FC shirt (yes, Chelsea, however hard that might be to believe) but, worse still, a *number nine* Chelsea shirt. And when that didn't bring about the desired resignation, it was revealed the pair of them had been ardent toe-suckers. 'It was just awful, awful, awful,' said the repentant Miss de Sancha later. 'It was complete and utter garbage.' But what are a few untruths between readers when the media bosses are intent on reforming the nation's morals? As the historian Macaulay said long ago, 'We know of no spectacle so ridiculous as the British public in one of its periodical fits of morality.'

Mr Mellor did ultimately resign, but not until late September and not because of the affair. The torpedo that finally sank him was a four-week holiday in the Spanish villa of a family friend, Mona Bauwens, the daughter of a fund-raiser for Yasser Arafat's Palestine Liberation Organisation. Unluckily for David, just as the holiday was in full swing, Saddam Hussein indulged another of his *folies de grandeur* and invaded

Kuwait. Britain went to war to help push him out, but the PLO was the only organisation that supported the invasion. The press, close to despairing of ever getting the Teflon-coated minister out of office, saw its chance of fighting on another tack, and this time it succeeded. 'Politically insensitive and possibly insulting to the citizens of British families,' thundered George Carmen QC, notorious for the insults he routinely dished out in court to British citizens unable to afford the fees that newspapers such as the *People* were able to pay him.

It was the end. Mellor was willing to fight on, but his fellow Conservatives were beginning to lose the will to back him, and this time his resignation was accepted. 'TOE-JOB TO NO JOB,' trumpeted the *Daily Mirror* triumphantly. The irony is that, nowadays, he makes far greater sums of money as a media man covering sport, music and the arts than ministers of the Crown or the editors of the *People* and the *Mirror* ever did.

'We Are Going To Have The Best-educated American People In The World'

Vice-President J Danforth Quayle Puts His Foot In His Mouth – Again (Trenton, 1992)

Dear Dan Quayle. What would America – and, for that matter, the rest of the English-speaking world – have done without him? He toyed with our rich language like a kitten with a mouse, but fortunately, like the cat in *Tom and Jerry*, could never quite finish it off.

Dan Quayle was a surprise nomination to run as vice-president on the Republican ticket in the 1987 presidential elections alongside George Bush Sr. Democrats were quick to portray the 42-year-old, who looked even younger, as dangerously inexperienced and ran ads showing a heart monitor below the words 'QUAYLE: JUST A HEARTBEAT AWAY.' Indeed, it was said much later that the presence of Quayle as VP was a guarantee that no one would ever attempt to impeach George Bush.

Nevertheless, Quayle managed to avoid any gaffes – linguistic ones, at least – during the election campaign, and had only one black moment. In a televised debate with his Democrat opposite number, Lloyd Bentsen, he made the mistake of comparing his own experience with that of John F Kennedy. 'Senator,' replied Bentsen, 'I served with Jack Kennedy. I knew Jack Kennedy. Jack Kennedy was a friend of mine. Senator, you're no Jack Kennedy.' It was a numbing put-down, but the ticket survived. George

Bush Sr swept to the presidency and Dan Quayle became the 44th vice-president of the USA, free to embark on his career of entertaining us with his use of the language.

Streetwise political commentators have assured us that Quayle was more politically savvy than his boyish face implied, but a stream of malapropisms made it seem distinctly otherwise. It was inevitable that, once these began, there would be no lack of wags to help him along with a few inventions of their own, and here one has to be careful in winnowing the real ones from the apocryphal. Did he, for example, really protest at the idea of a visit to Latin America because he didn't speak Latin?

We can, though, be sure of his biggest bloomer, which came towards the end of the Bush–Quayle period in office and centred on the humble potato. Ginger Rogers and Fred Astaire may have sung about calling the whole thing off because they couldn't agree on how to pronounce potato (not to mention tomato), but at least they could spell it. Dan, the nation discovered to its delight in 1992, could not.

Trenton, New Jersey is doubtless a splendid place, once you get to know it, but is not a destination that figures in the top one thousand preferred holiday spots. It's unlikely that Dan was humming cheerfully to himself as he embarked on a boring round of ritual handshaking with the worthy burghers of the town on 15 March as the re-election campaign began to warm up. That afternoon, he noted, he was to visit the local Munoz Rivera High School and watch a spelling bee in progress. This no doubt elicited an inward groan.

Come the appointed hour, Dan swept into the school with his aides and was handed a pile of cards on which had been carefully inscribed the words that were to be spelled by the students. 'Have these been vetted?' he whispered from the corner of his mouth. The answer was reassuring: everything was in order. No mention of Latin America, Democrats or the economy, stupid.

Twelve-year-old William Figueroa stepped up to the blackboard, chalk in hand, to be given his word from the vice-presidential mouth. 'Potato' came the call. William advanced to the blackboard and carefully inscribed p-o-t-a-t-o. The VP glanced at the card in his hand. 'You're close,' he quailed gently, 'but you left a little something off. The E on the end.'

It was Dan's bad luck that the teacher who had written out the cards was a shaky speller herself, and even worse that a local reporter turned up a few minutes later. 'Did he foul up?' he enquired hopefully, Did he foul up!

In no time the reporter was racing back to the offices of *The Trentonian*. Two hours later, Dan's hot potato hit the newsstands. The next morning, it was the lead item on breakfast-time TV across the US and people went to work with a spring in their step and a smile on their lips. Later that year, Bush and Quayle failed to be re-elected for a second term.

Dan Quayle had a shot at the Republican presidential nomination in 2000. In a straw poll in Iowa, he came eighth and withdrew from the race. But he left us with an anthology of sayings, some genuine, some probably not. Here's a sampler of a few that were recorded:

'We all lived in this century. I didn't live in this century.' (1988)
'Verbosity leads to unclear, inarticulate things.' (1988)
'We're going to have the best-educated American people in the world.' (1988)
'I stand by all the misstatements that I've made.' (1989)
'Quite frankly, teachers are the only profession that teach our children.' (1990)
'We are ready for any unforeseen event that may or may not occur.' (1990)
'Illegitimacy is something we should talk about in terms of not having it.' (1992)

. . . and these might not be genuine, but they're enjoyable all the same:

'The future will be better tomorrow.'
'Republicans understand the importance of bondage between a mother and child.'

'I love California. I practically grew up in Phoenix.' (Phoenix is in Arizona.)

'I am not part of the problem. I am a Republican.'

And, best of all:

'People that are very weird can get into sensitive positions and have a tremendous impact on our history.'

Quite so.

'Dear Boy, I Can't Get The Door Closed'

The Matrix Churchill Case (1992)

It was probably inevitable that, when Alan Clark was promoted by Mrs Thatcher to be a junior minister at the Department of Employment, his first speech in the Commons should be at the behest of Brussels in support of a bill outlawing sex discrimination. Not only was Clark outspokenly anti-feminist but he also reserved his deepest scorn for the European Union. Worse than that, the bill had to be piloted through the House during a late-night sitting, the full import of which was not lost on the opposition. The chance that Clark would have had a snifter or two was highly probable – indeed, he'd had nine or ten while sampling some fine wines and clarets somewhat earlier in the day – and he had most certainly not bothered to cast an eye over the papers thrust into his hands by the functionaries in his department. 'I found myself sneering at the more cumbrous and unintelligible passages,' he confided to the diaries he had every intention of publishing later. As official accounts like to record on such occasions, 'uproar ensued'.

Few were surprised, for Alan Clark was a contradiction in almost everything he did, believed in or stood for. He played the role of an aristocrat (which he was not) in a fifteenth-century castle that his family had purchased only in 1955. He was a (repeatedly) self-proclaimed Nazi who hated fascists (branding them 'shopkeepers who look after their dividends'), a bon viveur who was a vegetarian, a man of intolerable rudeness to those who bored him yet deeply and consistently concerned about the welfare of animals, and an outrageous sexist who nevertheless charmed (most) women and was full of admiration for Mrs Thatcher. He was, in fact, about as politically incorrect as it is possible to be and remain in public office, a fact that should endear him to more people than, strictly speaking, he deserves to be admired by.

Alan Clark's *Diaries*, when they appeared in the mid-1990s, were gloriously indiscreet and endeared him to another tranche of the population – although not to a gentleman in South Africa, who shall remain unnamed for the purpose of this book, who discovered that Clark had had simultaneous affairs with his wife and both of his daughters. He was not in the least amused and caught the first available flight to the UK in order to administer a horse-whipping that Clark agreed he deserved but declined to receive. It was therefore hardly surprising that, when Clark was asked during a television interview if he had any skeletons in his cupboard, he cheerfully replied, 'Dear boy, I can't get the door closed.'

Oddly, the diaries make no mention of the Matrix Churchill affair, to which Clark had an input that rather discomfited his own party. Mrs Thatcher accepted his many and varied misdemeanours with a good-humoured tolerance allowed to nobody else except, perhaps, the saintly Cecil (see p. 85). Perhaps she thought it a good idea to have a troublemaker close at hand to speak his unorthodox mind and embarrass those who too readily agreed with everything she said.

Be that as it may, in 1986 Clark found himself Minister of Trade and, three years later, Minister for Defence Procurement. At that time the Iran–Iraq war was in full and bloody swing and government guidelines clearly prohibited the export to either side of any material that could be used in the manufacture of arms. One firm that belonged to the MTTA (Machine Tools Trade Association) was Matrix Churchill, who were controlled by an Iraqi company. Clark let it be known in the MTTA that he wasn't much concerned if companies breached the guidelines. So they did – or, at least, Matrix Churchill did. When he moved on to defence procurement, he developed his theme, announcing, 'I am not particularly bothered about who we're trading with, providing we get paid.' This is known in the trade as taking a robust view. It was a view that wasn't universally admired, however, and as Iraq prepared to invade Kuwait in 1990, the *Sunday Times* became quite stroppy on the subject. And, as we see weekly, where one newspaper leads, the rest are bound to follow, like a pack of hounds after a fox, with the result that a couple of years later, three executives from Matrix Churchill found themselves on trial for deceiving officials at the Department of Trade and Industry. The prosecution witness statement had been signed by none other than Alan Clark. 'But this isn't fair!' wailed the three executives jointly and severally. That nice Mr Clark had said it was all right.

Nice Mr Clark entered the witness box and took the oath. Absolutely right, he boomed. I did say so, and I should have read the witness statement before signing it. All a ghastly cock-up.

The trial promptly collapsed, leaving a trail of deeply embarrassed Tories and civil servants picking themselves off the floor. Alan Clark was not among them. Showing not the least sign of repentance or, perish the thought, embarrassment, he retired to his castle and got on with his entertaining diaries, which were awaited by the denizens of Westminster with considerable trepidation.

Affairs Of State

MPs Caught With Their Trousers Down
(1993 And Passim)

Why pick 1993 when almost any year in the 1990s would have yielded similar stories of salaciousness? Because it was at the Conservative Party Conference in October of that year that John Major issued his clarion call to get 'back to basics'. He knew what he meant, and so did the party faithful: they needed to stop bickering among themselves, especially about Europe, and concentrate on those things that encouraged social cohesion, such as education, citizenship and respect for the law. His speech implied leadership of renewed vigour, and the delegates loved it. The media, however, chose to interpret it in a completely different way – as a self-righteous moral crusade announced by a party with a long pedigree of scandalous affairs of its own.

With the scent of David Mellor's blood still fresh in their nostrils (see pp. 103–106), not to mention the fun they'd had the previous year with the Liberal leader, Paddy 'Pantsdown' Ashdown, the gentlemen of the press stocked up on notepads and pencils. An experienced therapist and counsellor working for marriage counsellors Relate reckoned recently that 25%–30% of the British population have had or are having an affair. If they follow the national trend, that means that almost 200 of the 660-odd members (of parliament, that is) must also be guilty, so perhaps it's just as well that there's insufficient room in the Palace of Westminster for them all to have an office there or the place would be swaying on its foundations. It's therefore hardly surprising that in 1993 the fourth estate barely had time to sharpen its collective pencil before it was in action.

First into the lists was the irrepressible Stephen Norris, Minister of Transport and MP for Epping Forest, where, it was wrongly supposed, he had lived peaceably for nearly quarter of a century with his wife, Vicky. In point of fact, she had long since moved into her own house on the other side of London and was well aware of what 'him outdoors' got up to during the week – which, it later transpired, is more than could be said for the recipients of his ardour. Hugging themselves with glee, the tabloids were able to announce to a largely admiring readership that the minister had not one, not two, not three nor even four mistresses, but five! One for every working day of the week! Oh, joy. Oh, bliss! None of the mistresses, they said, knew about the other four until they, the intrepid reporters, had revealed it. As one commentator put it when Norris was running for Mayor of London in 2000, 'To have five mistresses on the go at once provides demonstrable evidence of organisational skills.'

Needless to say, it wasn't really quite like that – or, as the genial Stephen said, 'What appeared in the tabloids was considerably at variance with the facts, but there is no mileage for me in going into it.' The five mistresses were not simultaneous but sequential, stretching back over a 15-year period. There was (i) from 1978–86 a lady surgeon, succeeded by (ii) a sales executive, who flounced out in 1991 and was followed in rapid succession by (iii) a journalist, (iv) a publisher and (v) the secretary of a fellow MP. Despite the tabloids' best efforts, however, Stephen Norris was not forced to commit *hara kiri*; instead he cheerfully owned up and, seeing a likeable, forthright man, never given to striking censorious poses about other people, nobody really wanted his blood.

The ink was still fresh on Major's 'back to basics' speech when the tabloids, digging for dirt with the enthusiasm of a burrowing badger, came to the surface with another prize, this time in the shape of Tim Yeo. Like Norris, Yeo wasn't given to passing inflated moral judgements on others, but he had, with unfortunate timing, allowed himself to say in a speech to his constituency, 'It is in everyone's interests to reduce broken families and the number of single parents.' This seems an unexceptional statement, but it transpired that Mr Yeo hadn't exactly been doing his bit – at least, not in the direction implied by his speech. He had, in short, fathered a child that very year with a single mother. His wife knew all about it and then, as now, remained loyal to him. Moreover, it appeared that Yeo dealt considerately and thoughtfully with the single mother in question, herself a Tory councillor in a London division. At least she has never allowed herself to be dragged into the papers despite, one must presume, financial offers to do so. But Yeo made the mistake of trying to avoid the press by hiding from them rather than by disarming them with cheerful frankness as Norris had done, and in January 1994 he was forced to resign.

As the party in power and authors of the misbegotten 'back to basics' idea, the Conservatives were the natural target for the media, but there were also members of the opposition who were forced to hunt frantically for their trousers as the spotlight swung towards them. Liberal Paddy 'Pantsdown' had been one such victim, and 1994 was to catch a Labour member in its beam. To undisguised Tory glee, that member was none other than Dennis Skinner, the Beast of Bolsover himself – or, as the press happily renamed him, the 'Beast of Legover'.

The Beast made a very public virtue of living in the same council house he had always occupied with the same wife he had always had while castigating almost everyone around him – including, sometimes, members of his own party – with caustic gibes about their less than socialist habits and policies. Yet all this time, if the red-tops were to be believed (sorry, silly thing to say), the Beast had been having it away with a glamorous young Sloane Ranger in her Chelsea flat.

The truth, alas, was a little different. The lady in question was a middle-aged American, had been Mr Skinner's secretary and researcher almost for ever and, while it's true that she had a flat in Chelsea, it was no more than an over-sized broom cupboard. Nevertheless, the fearless publiciser of other people's shortcomings was said to take care to sidle up to his mistress's modest apartment with his hat pulled over his eyes and a woolly scarf disguising his features before settling into the undergrowth to await the all clear to enter. Ah, those were the days!

Business Is Suspended

Bill Clinton And The Lewinsky Affair (1995–8)

Once upon a time, so long ago it was in the last millennium, there lived in a faraway land a very important President called Clinton. Half his people loved him very much and called him Bill, and half of that half loved him even more than anybody guessed at the time. Bill lived in a palace called The White House. He had Hillary to keep him company. She was called First Lady and had a staircase all of her own. She was called First Lady because there were lots and lots of other ladies who went up and down another staircase to visit Bill, but nobody explained that to Hillary who thought she was the only lady. This may have been because she was so busy planning to be President herself one day that she didn't go up her special staircase to see Bill very often.

But although one half of his people loved him, some of them very much, the other half didn't love him at all, and they tried as hard as they could to find out wicked things about Bill. When he first became President in 1993 they found a powerful wizard or, as they are sometimes called, a lawyer, to see if he had done anything bad in something called Whitewater. The wizard's name was Ken Starr, and he hated Bill so much he spent years and years trying to cast spells over him, or litigation as lawyers called it, so he would vanish in a puff of smoke. Whitewater was a real estate venture in a corner of the faraway land named Arkansas, where Bill had been Governor before he became very important. He and Hilary had shares in Whitewater but sold them before the real estate venture lost all its money. Wizard Starr was sure something wicked must have been done because Bill and Hillary kept their money while everybody else lost theirs. He was in the middle of trying to prove this when someone whispered to him about all the ladies that went up and down the secret staircase to tell Bill how much everybody loved him. There was one called Paula Jones, they said. And he heard about another named, very aptly, Kathleen Willey who was seen coming out of Bill's office – when everybody thought he was working hard at saving the world, or at least America – 'looking dishevelled, her face red and her lipstick off'. Everyone knows it is very wicked indeed to look dishevelled and not have your lipstick on, and Wizard Starr was rather peeved, especially as none of these ladies ever came to see him with or without lipstick. Then he heard about one called Monica Lewinsky, and he could bear it no longer.

In 1995, Monica Lewinsky had spent a lot of time with Bill explaining to him how much everybody loved him for being such a good President, and naturally when you have such a big – er – job you like to hear these things from time to time. As Bill said, to one of his secret service men, Louis Fox, on one of these occasions, he could 'close the door because she'll be in here for a while'. Well, naturally. There's a lot to talk about. About a year later, Monica was chatting to a friend called Linda Tripp and discovered to her astonishment that she didn't like Bill. So she spent a lot of time explaining to her on a tape recorder what a good President he was so that Linda could listen to it at home and realise what she was missing. But naughty Linda was in the pay of Wizard Starr all the time. He listened to the tapes lots and lots of times and got very excited, but at last he came out of his office, probably looking rather dishevelled, and told everybody that Bill was not fit to be President because he was spending too much time with ladies who were not called First Lady. When Hillary heard this she became very angry, stamped her foot and said it was all 'a vast, right-wing conspiracy'.

Bill got pretty cross as well, because whenever he went on television (as he seemed to do every few weeks in 1998) and said 'I did not have sexual relations with that woman, Miss Lewinsky', half the country didn't know what he meant until they had looked it up in the dictionary and the other half didn't believe him. But they were all enjoying the story so much they asked him to keep on telling it. It reminded them of the bedtime tales their mothers' used to read them, and they couldn't wait for the next episode. Bill had been planning a war to stop terrorists attacking Americans in Kenya and Sudan as well as in New York, but he had to spend so much of his time telling stories that in the end he gave up running the country for a whole year. The odd thing was, the more stories he told the crosser Wizard Starr became, until in the end he made Bill appear before a Grand Jury.

Now Grand Juries are almost the only people in America who don't like listening to stories. They spend all their time asking difficult questions, and they nearly always know if you give the wrong answer. This was very difficult for Bill because they had got hold of a dress worn by Monica Lewinsky and on it was a stain that, they said, proved he had been discussing politics in bed with her. Moreover Hillary got pretty damn mad to discover that although she was called First Lady, Bill usually said he was too tired to discuss politics with her when they'd finished their cocoa and switched out the light. All in all it was a trying time for Bill, and in August 1998 he appeared on television again – because he was more entertaining than the soap operas Americans had used to watch – and explained that when he said he had not had sexual relations with Monica Lewinsky before, he didn't realise they meant *that* kind of sexual relations. He thought, as he looked back over things, that he might inadvertently have had a relationship that was – what could he say – inappropriate? That half of the people that hated him were thrilled to bits by this. You would often see them jumping up and down chanting 'impeachment', which is a magic curse. The other half, who were still pretty fond of him and were very grateful for all the entertainment he'd given them for a whole year, asked what difference any of this made to Bill's ability to run the country. As the two halves couldn't agree with each other they forgot the magic curse, and Wizard Starr had to sit huddled in a corner by the chimney grumbling to himself.

'I Am A Man Of Unclean Lips'

Jonathan Aitken sues the Guardian (1997–9)

As you might remember, we left Jonathan Aitken on page 72, his head ringing from Mrs Thatcher's steel-lined handbag and little prospect, it seemed, of political advancement. So you are naturally wondering, how did the wee charmer turn out in the end? I don't know quite how to break this, and those of a nervous disposition should perhaps turn to the next chapter because – and I know it sounds silly – he declared, 'I am a man of unclean lips,' and was promptly popped in the slammer. Honest! ('It will not be too bad for someone who has been at Eton,' he said, and indeed the comparison is probably quite apt.) And no, I don't know if it was because he smoked too many Saudi Arabian cigarettes or if it had anything to do with a flying handbag in 1976. It just happened that way. However, I can give you a few clues.

Mrs Thatcher never relented in her eleven and a half years in Number 10, during which time Jonathan had to plough on as a humble back-bencher. Soon after John Major got the keys of the front door, though, things changed and JA became Minister for Defence procurement in 1992 and then Chief Secretary to the Treasury in 1994, meaning he got to be in the Cabinet. Good stuff, and things going along swimmingly. Apparently. However, this is where the 'buts' begin to crop up, approximately in this order:

120

(a) he had become a non-executive director of defence manufacturing company BMARC for an eighteen-month period between 1988 and 1990. (Allegations would later surface that the company had engaged in illegal arms deals with Iran and Iraq, of which, it was said, Jonathan must have had some knowledge. This would muddy the waters as further events unfolded, not least because the Scott Inquiry was set up in 1992 to investigate the arms deals);

(b) throughout his period in the political wilderness under Mrs Thatcher, Jonathan had kept his contacts with the Saudis alive – indeed, the strength of his ties was a factor in his appointment as Minister for Defence Procurement;

(c) in September 1993, Jonathan was sighted in the Ritz Hotel, Paris, in the company of assorted Saudis. The bill for his stay, it was revealed very much later, was settled by Prince Mohammed bin Fahd;

(d) a month later, the *Guardian* was tipped off about this meeting by none other than much-publicised London shopkeeper and football club owner Mohammed al-Fayed (who happened to own the Ritz, Paris as well). When asked by the paper who settled the bill, Jonathan told them that the ever-loving Mrs Aitken (who later divorced him) picked up the tab;

(e) the *Guardian* obtained a fax of the bill that showed how it was paid, but elected to sit quietly on this revelation until a good moment came along in which to use it.

The good moment arrived in April 1995, the same month that Granada screened a documentary entitled *Jonathan of Arabia* about various personal and business dealings between Aitken and Prince Mohammed bin Fahd. These did not make for comfortable viewing in the Aitken household, and the *Guardian*'s revelation about the Paris hotel bill was the last straw. On

10 April, Jonathan resigned from the Cabinet in a blaze of righteous indignation and broadcast to the nation, 'It falls to me to start a fight to cut out the cancer of bent and twisted journalism in our country with the simple sword of truth and the trusty shield of fair play.' To the sound of trumpets, he issued a writ against the *Guardian* a fortnight or so later alleging defamation of character. For good measure, in December of the same year he issued another, this one linking Granada TV with the *Guardian* for all the unkind things they'd said about his time at BMARC.

The case came to court in June 1997. One month earlier Jonathan had lost his seat in the general election, so the year was already on course to becoming an *annus horribilis* for him. The following year turned out pretty badly as well, and, until God intervened, 1999 was the worst of the lot.

Jonathan's libel case against Granada and the *Guardian* collapsed in a heap when airline tickets were produced that proved no other member of his family could possibly have been in Paris at the time his wife was said to have paid the bill. This was swiftly followed by irrefutable evidence supporting the allegation that he had taken a commission on BMARC arms deals and concealed the fact from his own government colleagues as well as the press. In short order, Jonathan lost (i) all credibility, (ii) wife and (iii) Privy Council membership; but in 1998 he gained (iv) a writ for perjury, and (v) another one for perverting the course of justice. In 1999 he was convicted and invited to spend eighteen months at one of Her Majesty's United Kingdom R&R centres. Fortunately for him (if not the taxpayer), because the costs of his ill-advised onslaught on the *Guardian* and Granada TV left him bankrupt, the board and lodging came free.

In 1998, however, even before he'd been charged, Jonathan had reawakened an old source of comfort: his religious belief. This was not, to use his own words, 'a foxhole conversion', but something that had always been important to him. A year before he was sentenced, he had given a penitent address to the CS Lewis Foundation and the Prison Fellowship Ministry but prevented publication of it for fear of being seen as trying to influence the judge. In it he openly admitted to harbouring an excess of pride in being a cabinet minister, and that pride led him to 'impale himself on his own sword of truth'. He accepted that he deserved most of the vitriolic criticism that was heaped upon him for the lies he had told and insisted that he was deeply repentant. But, quoting from a book he'd read, he posed the conundrum, 'It needs a good man to repent, yet here is the catch. Only a bad person needs to repent; only a good person can repent perfectly. The worse you are, the more you need it and the less you can do it.' If that is the case, none of us has much hope.

Barking Mad (i)

The Sterile World Of Political Correctness And Risk Aversion (2000–present)

How much longer, you might be thinking, are we going to lie on our backs and put up with the narrow-minded and unthinking attitudes that are turning our society into one in which no-one trusts anybody, where even the mildest form of affection or appreciation is rejected in case it is misconstrued, and where all risk is eliminated? Politicians, our judiciary and the media must, in their separate ways, share the blame first for creating, then for enforcing beyond reasonable bounds and finally for failing to rein in the ogres of political correctness and health-and-safety enforcement before they run out of control.

Were you to explore the list of absurdities that the twin monsters of political correctness and risk aversion have thrown up in the last five years alone you could, with ease, fill a hefty volume. In the meantime, here is a random selection to keep you amused or, more likely, groaning at human stupidity.

In February 2002, the Director of Performance Management (and no, I didn't make that up) of Rotherham Health Authority decreed that Swinton Lodge, a nursing home in the area, must not use terms of endearment with its elderly residents unless written permission had first been obtained. So 'love', 'dear', 'sweetheart' and 'darling' are now officially (and officiously) banned there, despite the fact that these common and long-standing terms of endearment are particularly valuable in helping to reassure elderly folk who are frequently apprehensive at finding themselves dependent on others in residential care. But the Director of Performance Management, taking a breather to brush a speck of dust from the uniform and pin another medal to his or her chest, explained that these common terms of ordinary humanity and fellow feeling 'show lack of respect and take away the person's dignity'. No doubt you and I would love to believe that the DPM was sacked with ignominy for this cold and callous failure to understand real life in the corridors of a nursing home for the elderly, but I fear it is unlikely.

Lest you run away with the idea that such lunacy is confined to the north of England, Medway Council in Kent managed to make prats of themselves in 2005 when a woman decided to thank the staff for some helpful advice they'd given her by delivering a big bunch of daffodils to their office in person. 'We are sorry, madam,' droned the Medway prats, 'but we're unable to accept these, as they are politically biased.'

Very reasonably, the woman asked how flowers came to be politically biased. The answer, it seems, is that daffodils are yellow, the identifying colour of the Liberal Democrats.

So, there you have it: your garden is henceforth a political minefield. Red flowers, like roses and carnations, are out – Labour; blue, such as cornflowers or irises, are unthinkable – Tory; yellow, like daffodils and marigolds, are anathema – Liberal. Green is clearly out. We can't have people showing allegiance to the Green Party. So, if you're to be acceptably PC, you'll have to stick to bare earth and twigs or, better still, concrete the garden over.

As far as I know, not even Stalin, in his quest to massacre the population of the Soviet Union, ever thought of liquidating his subjects for growing flowers of the wrong colour. But Britain is the land of the petty civil servant who cannot rest until everything around him or her is reduced to a uniform grey. (Incidentally, what colour car do you drive? I'm sure you wouldn't want to offend your neighbour's political sensitivities.)

Next, consider everything we've done to ensure that our children grow up unable to cope with the real world of adult life. It would be nice to think that when, in 2002, a London primary school banned the making of daisy chains (no, I'm not joking; picking daisies brings you into contact with nasty dirty earth, in which might be lurking – shh! – *germs*), it provoked such howls of derision that the madness was quickly forgotten. It was not. On the contrary, it was followed in 2004 by the conkers ban.

In Clackmannanshire, Scotland, 'health officials' forced Menstrie Primary School to ban conkers in case nut-allergy provoked a reaction. 'You can't be too careful,' said the headmistress (a word I should not, of course, be using; if it's not too late, may I change it to headperson?).

Not to be outdone, the headmaster (a word that my legal team advises me is OK, though I confess to remaining apprehensive) of Cummersdale Primary School in Cumbria also banned conkers. 'You can't be too careful,' he told the press in a striking echo of the Menstrie headcreature, before adding hurriedly, 'especially when health-and-safety inspectors are watching.' Mercifully, he recognised that kids must be able to play something other that statues during breaktime and allowed conkers as long as they wore safety goggles. He bought two pairs of goggles to prove that he meant it, so form an orderly queue, kids, and wait your turn. After all, as the manufacturer of the goggles said, 'You can't wrap children up in cotton wool all the time.' Want a bet?

'So what else can we do to scare the living daylights out of our children?' asked *The Times* in the wake of the 'bonkers conkers' stories. Quite a lot, in fact. Just take a look at all the other things kids can't do these days. No running in the playground (you might trip and graze a knee), no skipping (use your common sense; you might fall over a rope) and, above all, no football (nasty, rough, *competitive* game, and your mother wouldn't want you to grow up like that Wayne Rooney, would she?). After all, as long ago as 2002, wise and farseeing Walsall District Council banned musical chairs in its playgroups in case it encouraged aggression among the toddlers.

You only have to turn around these days to find someone who wants to ban all competitive activity in schools, whether sporting or academic, in case someone is upset when they don't do as well as they claimed it was their right to do. It never occurs to them to ask how such mollycoddled children will fare when, as inevitably they must, they leave these sheltered nests to face an increasingly tough and demanding real world. Do they expect the American or Chinese businessman they are facing to make allowances for them because they weren't allowed to take risks at school? Or if – as many seem to want nowadays – they think they would like to become actors, do they expect to be given starring roles irrespective of whether or not they can actually act?

If you think these are silly questions, consider what happened when the Lancashire cricketer Chris Schofield appeared before an industrial tribunal in April 2005, claiming unfair dismissal. Professional sport is about as demanding as any performance-based activity gets, and in the 2004 season Schofield had taken precisely one wicket. His failure was among the reasons that his club, expected to be championship contenders, were relegated from the first division. This was no sudden loss of form; in the four seasons between 2001 and 2004, Schofield had taken a grand total of 39 wickets at the high average of 42.2 each – hardly the contribution a major county needs from its spin bowler when its business is to win matches. Yet, believe it or not, the tribunal panel asked Lancashire why they hadn't built up his confidence by playing him more often in the first XI. As ex-international cricketer and journalist Derek Pringle said, 'The riposte is perhaps best left to Homer Simpson: "Doh!"'

'Just A Villain Like The Rest Of Us'

Lord Archer Continues His Writing At Her Majesty's Pleasure (2000)

On 18 September 2005, al-Pieda struck again. Their victim on this occasion was Jeffrey Archer, or Lord Archer as he was known to a selection of prison governors whose hospitality he accepted between 2000 and 2003. Unless you keep your ear very close to the ground, you might not have heard of al-Pieda, but they are, in their own words, a 'political patisserie' devoted to promoting a 'global pastry uprising'. Their chosen weapons are custard pies, and they select their victims carefully, vetting them for pomposity, hypocrisy, oversized ego, any combination thereof, before striking.

Lord Archer was about to speak at a charity dinner in Manchester when an al-Pieda-flung custard pie found its target. The perpetrator fled giggling with cries of 'Monica Coghlan!' rending the air. The yet-to-be-defrocked peer was reported to be livid – but then, he would be; he seems to be a classic example of what Cornell University's Medical School calls ASN (Acquired Situational Narcissism), a self-love that is temperamental, egotistical and devoid of feeling for others.

But I should proceed with caution. After all, the noble lord has bounced back from disgrace with such regularity that, as one scribe in the *Scotsman* suggested not long ago, 'Give it five years and Jeffrey Archer will be a national treasure.' Who knows? If Britain decides to dispense with the monarchy, he might yet be the first president of the Republic of England, Wales, Bits of Scotland and Certain Parts of Belfast. This, therefore, is a bedtime story of how one of the country's literary giants *(sic)* came to be the target of a custard-pie thrower.

It all began when little Jeffrey was about four years old and told everybody that he wanted to be prime minister. He was an inventive child and soon found that he was very good at telling stories. With a little embroidery of the truth here, a spot of careful editing there and a good deal of ambition (mainly of the unclothed variety), he got along very well. There were some minor obstacles on the way; his life savings disappeared in 1974 after an unwise investment, forcing him to resign as an MP, and there was a careless moment in 1976 when he absent-mindedly took some coats from a Toronto store and accidentally forgot to pay for them. However, his gift for making up stories came in very useful in these situations and, even better, lots and lots of people paid to read them, so in what seemed like no time he'd made more money than he knew what to do with.

Jeffrey decided to go back into politics and, as he was now big and important – or, at any rate, rich – he didn't bother to get elected by a lot of scruffy people he didn't like. He worked out that politicians were really just like him and much preferred talking at parties (especially ones he was paying for) to big and important – or, at any rate, rich – people like him. Almost before you could recite the list of books he'd written, he found he was deputy chairman of the Conservative Party.

One day he picked up a newspaper called the *Daily Star* and read a story that said he had been having fun with a prostitute called Monica Coghlan. He got very cross when he read this because everyone in the Conservative Party knew that you only say such things in private to other members of the party and should never admit that you enjoyed it. This meant he had to resign as deputy chairman.

Jeffrey then paid Monica £3,200 to stay out of sight while he sued the *Daily Star* and persuaded his wife, Mary, to go into court, looking as graceful and fragrant as possible in order to put off the judge, Mr Justice Caulfield, in the hope that he would forget to listen to the embarrassing bits.

It worked. Lo and behold, the *Daily Star* was told to pay Jeffrey £500,000 and say sorry, which all goes to show that novelists are better at making things up even than newspapers. Best of all, the Conservative Party forgave him. In 1992 it said he could call himself Lord Archer, gave him a fluffy crown and told him to go and sit in the House of Lords and vote for them whenever he got the chance. This was a pleasant enough life, but became less attractive when Labour won the 1997 general election.

In 2000, Lord Archer decided that he'd rather like to be Mayor of London and announced that he would graciously permit the citizens, humble though they were, to vote for him. Not everyone thought this was a good idea, particularly his former secretary, and a friend who in 1987 had sworn (untruthfully) that he'd been with Jeffrey on the night that the *Daily Star* had accused him of being unable to spot the difference between Monica Coghlan and his fragrant wife.

In December 2000, they were all back in court and Jeffrey was invited to answer charges of perjury and perverting the course of justice. With considerable chutzpah, the noble lord managed to appear in the courtroom by day and by night in a play he'd written. *The Accused* was staged at London's Theatre Royal, with Jeffrey himself playing the title role, and the audience were invited to find him guilty or not, as they saw fit, at the end of each performance. The run of the play came to an abrupt halt, however, when the master storyteller was found guilty in the real court and went off to perform a somewhat longer run of three years behind bars. The MCC (Marylebone Cricket Club) was even crosser with him than the judge and suspended his membership of their organisation for seven years.

Nonetheless, Jeffrey still has some fans. One American writer who visited him in chokey said, 'I like him. He doesn't tell as many lies as Bill Clinton,' while one of his fellow time-servers reckoned, 'He wasn't such a bad bloke. Talked posh, of course, but he was just a villain like the rest of us.' Neatly put.

Barking Mad (ii)

Admiral Lord Nelson Falls Foul Of The Health And Safety Executive (1805 & 2004)

October 2005 saw the celebrations marking the bicentenary of one of Britain's most famous victories in adversity, the Battle of Trafalgar, fought off the Spanish coast. Faced with the threat of invasion by Napoleon, it was crucial to break French sea power and thwart Napoleon's attempt to ferry his army across the channel. Notwithstanding the susceptibilities of France (or the European Union, as our immediate neighbours prefer to be known), it was rightly felt that Trafalgar was something to be celebrated, even if Tony Blair and New Labour were unlikely to join in.

Try-outs and rehearsals began early, and towards the end of 2004 an actor dressed as Nelson posed for the cameras on the banks of the Thames at Greenwich. The next stage of the plan was for him to board an RNLI lifeboat and proceed down the waterway. Not so fast, muttered accompanying officials; little grey men from the Health and Safety Executive might be watching. So the would-be Nelson was obliged to proceed under full steam but clad in a yellow lifejacket that rather spoiled the intended effect.

Inspired by this latest piece of futile interference by mentally challenged bureaucrats, denizens of the internet promptly spawned a host of musings on the outcome of the Battle of Trafalgar had the Health and Safety Executive come into being (God help us all) two centuries ahead of time. I wish I knew the anonymous authors, but at least I can reproduce some of their comments in homage to them.

Imagine, then, that you're on the deck of Nelson's flagship, forcibly renamed HMS *Abject*. The conversation you overheard might run as follows:

'Send the following signal, Hardy. England expects that every man will do his duty. Got that?'

'Aye, aye, Admiral, though I fear I must make some slight adjustments. We're obliged to be an equal-opportunities employer now, sir. Message will therefore read, "England expects every person to do his duty, regardless of race, gender, sexual orientation, religious persuasion or disability." I should add, sir, that only with the greatest difficulty was I allowed to keep the word "England" in the signal.'

'Good God, Hardy! Well, put on all sail and give orders for full speed.'

'I'm sorry, Admiral, that won't be possible. We are in a restricted zone with a maximum speed of four knots.'

'Damn it all, Hardy! We're on the eve of the greatest battle in our history and you tell me I can't proceed to battle stations at full speed? Get someone up to the crow's nest at once to report on the position of the French.'

'I'm afraid that's impossible, my lord. The crow's nest is closed – orders of Health and Safety. There's no harness there, you see, sir, and they won't let anyone up there until there's full scaffolding around the mast. And while we're on the subject, sir, the rigging doesn't meet regulations and the crew have to wear hard hats before they can climb it. Oh, and before I forget, we have government-registered carpenters on board providing a barrier-free environment for the differently abled.'

' "Differently abled?" What kind of gobbledegook is that Hardy? What does it mean?'

'With respect, sir, it refers to people such as yourself. You've only got one arm, one eye and . . . well, one of most things, my lord, and it's to help you get around the ship.'

'Hardy, I've spent my life in the Navy and never had a problem getting anywhere, including to be admiral, so don't give me all that rubbish.'

'Begging your pardon, sir, it's hardly rubbish is it? I mean, ask yourself, would you really have got the top job if it hadn't been for the quotas? It could be that it's only because the Navy is short of men – excuse me, persons – deficient in limbs and eyesight that you got fast-tracked up the ladder.'

'This is too much, Hardy. I'm not allowed to know where the enemy is, I can't sail at the speed I want and now you're telling me I'm not fit for command. I've had enough. Order the cannon rolled out and primed.'

'Ah.'

'Ah?'

'I'm afraid I have to tell you that we can't have any shooting, sir. The men are afraid of being sued if they kill anyone, however accidentally. And we have the legal-aid johnnies on board touting for custom in case any of our chaps gets hurt and can be persuaded to blame it on someone else – such as you, sir – for giving them an order that, with careful hindsight, they decide might not have been in their own best interests. Especially if they can screw some taxpayers' money out of the deal. Sir.'

'Hardy, what on earth has got into you? This is war, Hardy! Our country is in grave danger of invasion. It's everyone's duty to get in amongst the French and blow them to pieces!'

'Oh, dear, dear, dear, sir. Do be careful what you say. These may be wooden walls, but they still have ears, sir, and we have a Cultural Diversity Co-ordinator on board. He really won't like that sort of language at all.'

'I give up, Hardy. Rum, sodomy and the lash; that's the Navy I joined. But it's not worth wasting my time for this lot.'

'I don't know, Admiral. It's not that bad. I know corporal punishment is out, and rum's not allowed any more, of course – the PM doesn't like binge-drinking if he's not the one doing it. But look on the bright side, sir; sodomy's very fashionable these days.'

'Oh, very well, Hardy. What is there to lose? Come on and kiss me, baby.'

And In The Red Corner, Two-Jags Prescott!

The Deputy Prime Minister Fights The 2001 Election Campaign – Literally

Once every four or five years, the British government of the day remembers with dismay that it has to try to get itself re-elected. It therefore steels itself to the unpleasant ordeal of leaving the tiny world of Westminster in order to spend a month pretending to like the millions for whose collective good it is supposed to govern. It's the one chance ministers have during those four or five years to meet real people, as opposed to media folk and other politicians, and find out what the country *really* needs in order to function smoothly. Come election time, one might expect them, therefore, to be on their best behaviour, smiling when their minders hiss, 'Smile!' in their ears and at all other times attempting to arrange their features into a semblance of geniality. In the 2001 election campaign, some of them did try, but, as usual, John Prescott was not, as they say, on message.

Nobody knew quite why John Prescott was in the government at all but, as a rare and exotic creature within New Labour's ranks (to whit, an ex-trade unionist) most presumed it must be to try to fool Old Labourites into thinking all must be well if good old John was there to keep smoothie Blair in order. Whatever the reason, there he was, so they put him in charge of one of New Labour's really exciting – I mean, hey, really important – new ideas: an integrated transport policy that would solve Britain's chronic lack of, well, transport. Good old John spent the first two years telling everyone what a fantastic policy it would be when he'd thought of it and the next two getting cross if anyone asked him if it was nearly ready.

Then the 2001 election was called, saving him from having to admit that he hadn't actually done anything at all apart from drawing his ministerial salary and enjoying the two his an' hers Jaguars that Mr and Mrs P insisted on owning, despite the availability of a chauffer-driven car at Westminster. For this the tabloids christened him 'Two Jags'.

There was one other thing entrusted to good old John. Every August, he was allowed to be the government spokesman when the prime minister was on holiday. He got very excited by this, largely because no-one had ever explained to him that nothing is allowed to happen in August as almost the whole country, including most journalists and all of his colleagues, is also on holiday.

So the 2001 election got under way and Two Jags set off to do his bit in the 'Prescott Express' battle bus – or 'blunderbuss', as it soon became known. The last thing any of the control freaks masterminding New Labour's campaign wanted was to let Mr P loose in the electoral heartlands, so they suggested that he went to see how things were getting along in north Wales, an area in which very few people lived, compared to most of Britain, and where it seemed unlikely that he could get into much trouble.

They were wrong. The heckling began as soon as the blunderbuss drew up outside the Little Theatre in Rhyl – not, you would have thought, a town famed for riot and affray. A group of about 25 protestors was demonstrating on the other side of the road, one of them waving a banner reading, 'AVERAGE FARMING WAGE IN WALES £75 A WEEK'. Two Jags levered his not inconsiderable frame out of the bus and pointed in their direction, whereupon an egg (uncooked) sailed out of the mini-crowd and scored a bullseye on his neatly tailored suit.

Now, eggs – preferably rotten ones – have been the common currency of street politics ever since Gladstone went on the stump in the nineteenth century, but this was something else that no one had thought to explain to Two Jags. Mindful, perhaps, of the way in which American presidents and vice-presidents such as Spiro Agnew, Gerald Ford and George Bush Sr have regularly decimated members of their electorate on the golf course by targeting them with wayward drives, he sailed in among the protestors. Correctly identifying the miscreant egg-thrower, he let loose with a haymaker, whereupon what journalists like to describe as a scuffle took place as the two men rolled around on the ground, clawing at each other. Another five protestors attempted to approach this most tempting of targets, but – alas for them – the police stepped in after ten seconds, evidently believing that this was about the right length of time that a member of the public should be given in which to try to throttle an out-of-condition politician.

Back at control headquarters in London, the campaign managers scarcely had time to bury their heads in their hands before more headline-making trouble broke out. Not only had the crowd of protestors swelled alarmingly – from 25 to a massive 30 – but around the corner came a convoy of approximately a hundred cars, lorries and tractors, honking loudly and protesting the price of fuel.

It was all too much. The curse of Two Jags had struck again, and there was nothing for the campaign managers to do but to pack him off on holiday somewhere, anywhere, as long as it wasn't in Britain.

Mr Prescott, meanwhile, was blithely unrepentant and totally unperturbed. Indeed, he gave the impression of having thoroughly enjoyed himself – as, indeed, he probably had. This, after all, was the man who would go on to decree the concreting over of what few green spaces were left in southeast England and declare in ringing tones, 'It was Old Labour that created the Green Belt and it's New Labour that's going to build on it.' Mr P might have very little clue about how to run a country, but at least he understands his primary duty as Deputy Prime Minister and keeps us thoroughly entertained.

Chirac Takes French Leave

Jacques Chirac Calls A Referendum On The EU Constitution (2005)

On French TV there is a popular satirical show titled *Les Guignols de l'Info* that features latex puppets, one of whose stars – to the joy of at least half the population – is a likeness of President Jacques Chirac. His character is constantly finding itself confronted by questions about his past that are too embarrassing to answer or trying to avoid uncomfortable political probings. When it's all becoming too much to bear, the Chirac puppet is transformed into its alter ego, SM ('Super Menteur'), a caped crusader reminiscent of Superman that tells the most outrageous lies and makes the most extreme promises without batting an eyelid. Super Menteur is French for 'Super Liar'.

It was Louis XIV, the Sun King, who in the seventeenth century solemnly pronounced, 'L'état, c'est moi,' which translates as 'I am the state' – ie 'I am France.' From time to time ever since there have been Frenchmen convinced that those privileged to look upon them were gazing at the personification of France itself. One such was Napoleon, and it cannot be denied he had leadership qualities, while Charles de Gaulle was another, although he earned his right by restoring French pride during World War II.

Then there was Jacques Chirac. Elected President in 1995, it took him only two years to demonstrate the quality of his political judgement. With a comfortable right-wing majority in the National Assembly, and with three years to run before fresh elections to it were required, he dissolved it.

137

Astute observers searched for reasons to explain this odd manoeuvre, but could discern none. His party lost the ensuing Assembly elections, and the five remaining years of his presidential term produced nothing but argumentative stalemate. He was re-elected for a second term as president in 2002, but this was largely because disillusioned right-wing supporters switched to Jean-Marie Le Pen's extreme-right party, Front National, to such an extent that they outvoted the socialist Left. In the required run-off vote, those to the left of centre were forced to vote for Chirac in order to keep Le Pen out. They did not easily forgive Chirac for putting them in so invidious a position.

Safely returned to the Elysée Palace, Chirac spent a couple of years hatching his next cunning plan, which he unleashed in 2005, no doubt while humming 'La Marseillaise'. A new European Constitution had been drawn up in Brussels. Strictly speaking, a referendum in the EU member countries was not required – Greece and Germany, for example, merely ratified the constitution in their parliaments. M Chirac, however, convinced in his own mind that he was the *de facto* emperor of Europe, thought it would be nice to have his own people acknowledge his supreme position by saying so in a referendum. Better still, his arch-enemy across the channel, Tony Blair, had announced a referendum in Britain. The wretched Anglo-Saxons would be sure to vote no, so a triumphant yes vote in France would ensure Britain's isolation in Europe while confirming Chirac's own position as The Main Man.

With a little less hubris and a better memory, M Chirac might have recalled that, when France had held a referendum on the Maastricht Treaty back in 1992, the yes vote had prevailed only by the narrowest possible margin. On this second occasion, on 29 May 2005, the no vote was a massive 55 per cent.

It was a humiliating drubbing for The Man Who Would Be France because, although there were many differing and sometimes contradictory reasons contributing to the rejection of the Constitution, one factor seemed to unite the no voters: dislike and mistrust of their president.

Fate had not finished with Jacques, however. The second instalment of his masterplan for 2005 was to be the bringing of the 2012 Olympics to

Paris, a contest for which France was odds-on favourite, this being their third such application. It was therefore a clear case of foot-in-mouth disease for M Chirac when a reporter overheard him giggling to his mate Gerhard Schroeder, the German chancellor, that, 'After Finland, Britain is the country with the worst food.' Pleased with this glittering witticism, he then questioned the mental capacity of English cows, observing that 'The only thing the English have ever done for European agriculture—' (forgetting, among other things, the invention of the seed drill) '—is mad-cow disease.'

Now, British cattle are well known for their equable temperament and ability to take a joke, but insulting Finnish food was another matter altogether, especially as Finland had two votes to contribute to the destiny of the 2012 Olympics. And yes, you've guessed it – on 6 July, London pipped Paris to the post for the 2012 Olympics by four votes, two of which, had they gone the other way, would at least have secured a tie. Needless to say, it wasn't the mayor of Paris who copped the blame back in France but good ol' JC himself. Oh, well. Maybe 2006 would turn out better.

Am-Bushed By A Hoover

George W Bush Gets Caught In The New Orleans Flood Disaster (2005)

The passage of Hurricane Katrina across New Orleans and Louisiana in September 2005 was not unexpected. Weather satellites gave ample warning of extreme conditions heading across the Gulf of Mexico, and everyone knew this hurricane was of above average ferocity. Some were warning that, if it hit low-lying New Orleans – as seemed probable – the banks, or levees, that were supposed to protect the city from the waters of the Mississippi River might not be strong enough.

On this occasion, the doom-mongers were proved tragically correct. New Orleans and surrounding towns were overwhelmed and suffered heavy loss of life. The city was rendered uninhabitable in a matter of hours, with survivors stranded on rooftops or in attics as the rising waters around them became steadily more polluted by the contents of ruptured sewage, gas and fuel pipes. Bodies floated in the streets and inside the houses where they had become trapped. Those survivors able to get there gathered in the New Orleans Astrodome and waited for help to arrive. For five days the only sign of external movement was provided by patrols of police (those that had not deserted) hunting and shooting looters. Then, with painful slowness, help began to arrive, unco-ordinated as it was to begin with. Nobody seemed to be in charge.

What, in the meantime, was President George W Bush doing to organise relief? Ever alert in an hour of crisis, on around the third day after the hurricane had struck he slipped into his best suit, rummaged in the wardrobe to find a smart tie and took a made flight to a patch of dry ground well away from the city. There he rallied the nation by wrapping his arms round a knot of survivors from towns outside New Orleans while the TV cameras rolled. It wasn't long before the swell of criticism at his failure to respond rose to a roar from within and without America.

Those with a sound grasp of history recalled Washington's very different response to an almost identical catastrophe in 1927. Then, as now, the New Orleans levees 'melted like sugar' and inundated the city, and film exists that shows a disaster very similar in scale to that which struck in 2005. Then, as now, those trapped were largely black and poor, lacking the means to escape.

The difference between the two calamities was that, back in 1927, the White House had responded immediately. President Calvin Coolidge despatched his Secretary of State for Commerce, Herbert Hoover, to organise relief. 'The Master of Emergencies', as he was soon dubbed, was not the kind of inward-looking American who lacked experience of the world; he had lived and worked in China, Australia and Europe, and during World War I he had rapidly set up an organisation in London that was effective in sending food and aid to Belgians trapped behind German lines. He was also notable for refusing a salary for any public office he occupied. Even when the law required him to accept one as Secretary for Commerce, he distributed it among charities and to those who worked for him whom he considered underpaid.

No sooner had Hoover arrived in New Orleans than he was to be seen – and photographed – striding through the waterlogged streets in thigh-length rubber boots, inspecting the problems at first hand. In no time, or so it seemed, he had called up the US Army, Navy, Coast Guard and the Red Cross and co-ordinated their efforts. Tent cities were established on the dry ground beyond the city, accommodating nearly 700,000 people in total, and these encampments were properly sanitised, policed and supplied with food and water. It was a Herculean achievement, and Hoover rightly took great credit for his organisational efforts and energy. Nevertheless, he was a politician, and there was a presidential election on the horizon, so, despite his hectic schedules, he made sure that cameramen had full access to what he was doing, and their efforts resulted in the first campaign film in history.

It paid off handsomely. Herbert Hoover, 'the Master of Emergencies', rode a crest of admiration all the way to the Republican nomination for President. It was more than a nomination ceremony; it was an enthronement. As he made his way to the stage to receive his acclamation, one radio commentator – his brain no doubt buzzing with the campaign slogan 'Who but Hoover?' – was so excited that he cried, 'Here comes the next president of the United States, Hubert Heever!'

As he ascended the throne, Hoover told the waiting masses, 'We are nearer to the final triumph over poverty than ever before in the history of any land.' But fate is no respecter of past achievement, however great and good it might be, and Hoover's presidency was barely a year old when disaster again struck America. The effects of the Wall Street Crash in 1929 were greatly compounded by the collapse of the European economy in 1931, and soon the Great Depression was well and truly under way.

Faced with the misery of lost jobs, homes and farmsteads, of lines waiting at soup kitchens, and of the hopelessness of beggars asking, 'Buddy, can you spare a dime?', the American people needed a scapegoat, and who could be more culpable than the president? It became common-place to accuse Hoover of doing nothing, whereas in truth he was attempting a great deal. It was Hoover who launched the Finance Reconstruction Company to get companies back on their feet, Hoover who demanded $400 million from Congress to increase Federal building programmes and Hoover who set up home-loan discount banks to help people to buy back their homes and farmsteads. Unlike the Louisiana floods of 1927, however, the Great Depression wasn't a catastrophe that could be localised and overcome in a few months. For Hoover, time began to run out, and in 1932 Franklin Delano Roosevelt and his 'New Deal' – a programme of economic and social reform – were swept into power.

For the New Deal to stand a chance of working, central government had to acquire and exercise power in ways to which America was unaccustomed. As Hal Barger noted in his book *The Impossible Presidency*, Roosevelt 'shifted the balance of policy initiative from Congress to the presidency', a move against which Hoover warned from the sidelines, even as he watched it happening. The irony is that, when Hurricane Katrina struck New Orleans over seventy years later, in 2005, the incumbent president, now holding centralised powers on a scale unimagined in 1927, seemed less able to rise to the challenge of providing immediate aid and organisation than Hoover and the Coolidge administration had been.

Hoover's standing with the public was raised sky-high in 1927, only to be destroyed a few years later. George W Bush's approval rating with the American public plunged to new lows after Hurricane Katrina. But what, in the longer term, does fate have in store for him?

It's A Dog's Life

David Blunkett And Sadie Are Forced Out Of Office, Not Once But Twice (2004–5)

You have to feel sorry for David Blunkett's guide dog, an affectionate and uncomplaining black Labrador named Sadie. Life was very comfortable when her master had a big room in the Home Office with plenty of civil servants there to bring her dog biscuits, and whenever they went to the Commons, where her master sat on the front benches, there was plenty of room to stretch out for a snooze, even though it sometimes got so noisy she had to put her paws over her ears.

Sadie is an easy-going, apolitical sort of dog, unlike her predecessor, Lucy, who once got so cross at the unkind things her master's opposite number was saying that she was sick all over the floor. Her master was very pleased and patted her on the head, joking about the airy-fairy libertarians on the other side of the House talking a load of dog's dinner, and all the people sitting behind him waved their arms around and laughed for a long time at this very witty joke. Odd people, these humans.

In those days, life for Sadie was full of variety. When her master had finished in his big office, they'd often go for long walkies (or sometimes in a car, if his needs were pressing) to see a lady named Kimberly Quinn. When they got there, he nearly always seemed rather tired and had to get into Kimberly's bed. Being a dog, and therefore always ready to curl up, Sadie could understand this and sometimes jumped up beside him, which seemed to make the lady quite cross.

One day, Sadie woke up to hear them talking about a nanny named

Leoncia and visas and fast tracks and special treatment, but as she didn't hear any magic words like 'supper' or 'walkies', she went back to sleep. The next thing she knew, there were reporters and photographers all over the place, and she and her master were off in a car to see a man named Tony. She liked Tony because he let her sit on the sofa next to him and tickled her ears, while he gave her master a handkerchief to wipe his tears away saying, 'Yuh, look, I mean, you know you have my full backing and complete confidence, David.'

That seemed to do the trick, because life suddenly got much more peaceful. Sadie no longer had to spend all day sitting in the big office, and whenever they went to the Commons she squeezed into a narrow space between the benches at the back, where it was more difficult to stretch out properly. And there were no more long walkies to see Kimberly Quinn. In fact, her master seemed to get very cross and bad-tempered whenever people mentioned her name, which they were always doing. He spent hours on the phone talking to horrid people from the newspapers and telling them she wouldn't let him see his son and that she'd even said it was someone else's. It all got quite boring for Sadie, who wasn't sure a puppy was worth all that fuss. She had always believed that you gave them a lick, a few drops of milk and then pushed them out of the door to sort things out for themselves. Odd people, these humans.

Then everything changed again. Now she and her master often visited a place she'd never been before, called DNA Bioscience, where he had become a director but where they practically never remembered to give her any biscuits, let alone a bone. One time there, she saw her master get out his chequebook and write in it, getting something called 'shares' in return.

One night, the men at DNA Bioscience took them both off to a place called Annabel's, where they drank a lot and her master met another lady, named Sally Anderson. She seemed very friendly, and the long walkies after work began again. Best of all, Tony phoned to say he was having an election, and when he won it her master could have a big office back and sit on the bench at the front again. Sadie was very excited, and for a month she and her master went all over the country, where there were lots of lampposts to sniff while he talked to crowds of people he'd never met

145

before. At last, he patted her on the head and said, 'We've won. Now we can go back to London for another five years.'

Back in London, life went on just as it used to before Kimberly Quinn, nannies, visas and fast tracks had spoiled everything. Her master was now called the Secretary for Work and Pensions and his new office wasn't quite as grand as the old one in the Home Office had been, but he seemed happy. He was allowed to sit on the front bench again, with plenty of room for Sadie to sleep so she didn't have to listen to his speeches and, especially, his jokes. Even so, she felt pretty mad with Lord Stevens, who had once been head of the police in London and who nearly accused her of sending stories to the press. 'There were only three of us in that office: myself, Mr Blunkett and his dog,' said Lord Stevens. 'And [the leak] didn't come from his dog.' Of course not. There were no lampposts in that office.

Then, without any warning, it was back to the quiet life and that narrow space between the back benches. What, in the name of a dog's hind leg, had he gone and done now? Apparently there was something called the 'advisory committee on business interests', whose members advised you to advise them about things like shares and directorships, so they can advise MPs with high blood pressure before they get over-excited because the media found out first. They were upset because her master hadn't advised them about something. But he didn't seem very worried about this until something terrible happened.

That nice man Tony rang up and said he wasn't to worry because he, Tony, was giving him his full backing and complete support, just as he had done for his friends Peter Mandelson and Stephen Byers. Sadie had never seen her master turn grey before, but she knew what it meant as he called his assistant and began to dictate his letter of resignation. It's a human's life, she thought, as she curled up and went back to sleep.

An Embarrassing Leak At The Security Council

President Bush Can Scarcely Contain Himself (15 September 2005)

The strain was showing on the President's face as he sat in the United Nations Security Council whilst it debated one of the pressing problems of the modern world – terrorism. This was the man who, only four years earlier, had warned the *New York Times* that 'redefining the role of the United States from enablers to keep the peace to enablers to keep the peace from peace-keepers is going to be an assignment'. Behind him in the Security Council, helping him to figure out what he meant, sat John Bolton, American Ambassador to the UN, and Condoleezza Rice, George Bush's Secretary of State.

As Prime Minister Tony Blair stood droning ever onwards at the podium, the President fiddled anxiously with his papers and pursed his lips, his eyes glazed. His thoughts went back to the way he'd been hijacked on his way to the chamber only two hours earlier by that wretched man John Howard, claiming to be prime minister of somewhere he'd never heard of. Australia, he might have said. Or was it Austria? It began with an A, and he was pretty sure it wasn't in America. This Howard fellow had grabbed him by the sleeve and begun gabbling about something called 'the Ashes'. Apparently, the Brits had walked off with them only three days earlier and Howard wanted the UN to demand their return to Australia, or Austria, or wherever the damn fool came from. Otherwise he'd have to vote the other way, he said.

147

What on Earth had Bush's old pal Tony Blair been up to now? Why couldn't even he be trusted? He had asked Condoleezza – good old Condy, who was always there to tell him what he ought to say – what these Ashes were, and even she had no idea. She thought it might be to do with something called 'cricket', because it had been impossible to get anyone in England to answer the phone for weeks because of it, but she wasn't sure. If it hadn't been for John Howard stopping him on his way to the debate, he wouldn't be in this goddam predicament now.

He sat there, trance-like, considering the courses of action open to him. Surrounding delegates glanced anxiously at his tense, drawn face. What was America up to now? they asked themselves. Was the president planning to tear down the UN building on New York's fashionable East Side and redevelop it as a shopping mall? Where would they end up if he did? And what would they do for restaurants if he sent the UN to upstate New Jersey?

At last, the President reached a decision. Brusquely, he reached for his pencil and scribbled a note to Condy. Good old Condy would know what to do. He slipped it to her surreptitiously. She pored over it apprehensively, frowning in concentration. 'I think I may need a bathroom break. Is this possible? W, the missive read.' Dr Rice clucked softly under her breath in sympathy. She had often heard that ordinary mortals were sometimes afflicted in these unexpected ways, and it added to her experience of learning to live among them. She whispered in her boss's ear and a peaceful look came over his face.

Her advice, it was later revealed, was to cross his legs hard and think of baseball until his old pal Tony Whatshisname had finished speaking. It would, after all, look bad if he seemed to be staging a walkout while Tony was doing his soft-cop spiel. Then he and John Bolton could both go and seek relief, because the next speaker was President Kerekou of Benin, and lots of other people were bound to have the same idea. Just to be on the safe side, though, she, Condy, would slip into the president's chair while he was gone so nobody would think his departure was official. And anyway, it would be good practice for when she became president, before she returned to her own planet.

And so it came to pass that George W Bush was free to make a dash for the gents. Well, not a dash, exactly, for there was security to be considered. While he waited with firmly crossed legs, the President's Secret Service bodyguards inspected the premises – dear God, there are times when you wish these guys wouldn't be so thorough – but at last they were able to report the deeply reassuring news that the label on the door reading 'GENTS' was genuine. There were 'no windows, one way in, one way out, and two stalls' – presumably, one for the US ambassador to the UN and the other for the president. Fortunately, things weren't so bad that he needed more than one.

The media hounds being what they are the President's mercy dash made immediate headlines. Medical experts were consulted to pronounce upon a matter that is, for the remaining billions of us who have yet to be appointed delegates to the Security Council, a rather familiar experience. It was a relief, if you'll forgive the double entendre, to learn that, 'In older men, it is unwise to delay passing urine when there is a strong need to, as there is a risk of developing acute urinary retention.' Older men? Why be so selective? This must be the only statement in the history of mankind with which every person on the planet concurs.

Labour Rebels 1 (A Blair, og), Prime Minister 0

Tony Blair Fails To Force His Anti-terrorism Bill Through Parliament (2005)

Hey, babes and cronies. Tony speaking. You know how you've often heard me telling you we've got to take Africa seriously. I mean, you know, I've been banging on about it for years, and there's a good reason. Those guys in Africa can really teach us a thing or two about leadership. There's Mugabe, of course, although being a bit short of food he doesn't have many people left to lead. And I've just finished reading a biography of Idi Amin in Uganda. Bit before my time, of course, but as he said himself, you could hear de smack of firm gu'mment in Kampala from as far away as Entebbe – or the splash of clear water as the opposition got thrown to the crocodiles. Pity there are no crocodiles in the Thames; I wouldn't mind tossing Bob Marshall-Andrews and the rest of my backbench clothheads off the terrace of the House . . .

Where was I? Yes, firm leadership, of the kind I showed you all in my first two terms when my majority was so big I could rule unchallenged from number ten. That's what the country wants – or needs, at any rate – and if only you'd voted me another thumping majority in May 2005 instead of an unworkable sixty we wouldn't be in this mess now with my anti-terrorism bill.

It was a good bill, really good, full of things to get us on the front foot in putting people away who don't think I'm right – about terrorism, I mean but, hey, it's an attractive thought. I particularly liked the bit about nicking those liberal woollies who glorify terrorism. That chap in the Commons who said I'd have to have Cherie banged up might be on to something. She hopes I've forgotten what she said in 2002 – 'as long as young people feel they have got no hope but to blow themselves up you're never going to make progress' – but she knows jolly well I haven't. I made her apologise at the time, and I keep reminding her to keep her mouth shut. Makes breakfast time pretty uncomfortable, I can tell you, but you have to put up with these things if you're a born leader. Now she's started going on about education. Keeps muttering that if it hadn't been for our educational system she'd have ended up a shop girl instead of a high court judge. Well, I nearly made the obvious comment, but I didn't want kipper all down my tie. Anyway, what she doesn't know is that I've got an education bill up my sleeve that should make sure there are no more like her if it gets through. I mean, we need shop girls, yuh? How's the economy going to survive if we can't sell things made in China to tourists?

Ninety days for the police to question terrorists – er, sorry, suspects – that's all I wanted. The police assured me they couldn't get any worthwhile information in less, and if they don't know the answer, who does? As good old Charlie Clarke said, if you're ill, you do what the doctor tells you; if the police beat you up, there's always a lawyer touting for business. So, it stands to reason – if someone other than a cop's got it in for you, you want the police. It's so obvious I'd have thought even the Tories could see that. After all, they always used to be the ones shouting that we didn't have enough flogging and keelhauling. But – would you believe it? – they didn't like ninety days. Said it was much too long and would only turn innocent people into disaffected martyrs and make them want to become terrorists.

Have you ever heard anything so ludicrous? I mean, look, think about it: the police wouldn't arrest them in the first place if they were innocent, and if they end up after ninety days wanting to blow up themselves and a lot of other people, it just shows we need more than ninety days, not less. I don't know what the Tories are coming to these days. They don't really care, as long as they can make me look silly. But they had reckoned without my inspiring gifts of leadership.

I've read the opinion polls, and I know the people of Britain want at least ninety days. So I worked out that the louder I said, 'Ninety days!', the more the Tories would stick to the fourteen days we already had or, at the very worst, twenty-eight. Unlike me, they weren't clever enough to realise that this simply made them seem weak and weedy in the eyes of the electorate, who would start saying that I – I mean we – are now the Party of Law and Order. Foolproof!

All Charlie Clarke and the whips had to do was explain to our side that this wasn't really a debate about terrorism at all but about scoring a big hit on the Tories. Sure, a few people might get banged up for ninety days in the process, because you can't expect Scotland Yard to understand anything as complicated as politics, but, hey, listen: I've watched *Blackadder* too, and I yield to no one in my admiration for some of Baldrick's cunning plans. I reckon I'd come up with something even he wouldn't have thought of that demonstrates my leadership skills to the full.

The trouble is, since the last election, Westminster's become an ungovernable rabble. The more the whips explained the plan to our own stroppy lot, the more confusing it all became. Even I struggled to keep up with all the numbers flying about. There was the fourteen days we've already got, but then everyone started running around spouting figures: 28, 30, 42, 60 – almost anything but good, law-abiding ninety. Poor old Charlie had to go around pretending he might compromise on some other number. Two days before the vote in the Commons, he even went on television to say that he thought a compromise was a workable idea and he would put all the numbers in a hat, shake them up and settle for the first one he pulled out (provided it wasn't 14, 28, 30 or 42). The trouble is, ever since I made him Home Secretary, Charlie has been a bit impetuous and he'd forgotten to ask me first, so an hour or two later I had to tell him to go back on TV and say I'd decided – I mean, we'd decided – that it was ninety days or nothing. The whips said it would be all right because they'd keep reminding Bob Marshall-Andrews and the other rebels they were *New* Labour now, however much they didn't like it, and that meant doing what they were told. And anyway, they'd be so pleased to see the bottom drop out of the Tories' opinion-poll ratings that they'd forget all about letting the police get their hands on a few troublemakers for ninety days.

Just to be on the safe side, we called all our heavyweights back to base. Poor old Gordon Brown had only just stepped off his plane to Israel when he had to climb back in and head for home, meaning he had to drink his duty free on the return leg or pay duty, which is bad economics; John Reid was hauled out of the British Embassy in Washington and bundled onto a plane before he could say 'CIA'; and Jack Straw had to be tracked down somewhere in Russia. As you can imagine, none of them was in the sunniest of tempers, and I could tell from Gordon's distracted look that he was thinking about the new carpets he'd be wanting in Number 10.

The next thing I knew, there were more figures flying around; 322 was one and 291 was the other. Surely, I can't have lost? With my leadership skills? Damnation! That means I've got about ninety days before Gordon starts moving all the furniture out of Number 11.

Hey, listen. I've just had a great idea. What with global warming and everything, we should introduce crocodiles into the Thames . . .